STACY GREGG grew up training her bewildered
dog to showjump in the backyard until her parents gave
in to her desperate pleas and finally let her have a pony.
Stacy's ponies and her experiences at her local pony club
were the inspiration for the *Pony Club Secrets* books, and
her later years at boarding school became the catalyst
for the *Pony Club Rivals* series.

Pictured here with her beloved Dutch Warmblood
gelding, Ash, Stacy is a board member of the Horse
Welfare Auxiliary.

Find out more at: www.stacygregg.co.uk

D0113337

The Pony Club Rivals series:

Coming soon...

PONY CLUB RIVALS
Riding Star

STACY GREGG

HarperCollins *Children's Books*

Riding Star *is dedicated to my riding instructor, the wonderful Nicola Ward, and to Kirsten Kelly who looks after my horse so well whenever he's at 'boarding school'. Also my equine support group: Sandra Noakes, Nicky Pellegrino, Fiona Curtis and Gwen Brown. I wrote the last chapters of this book in Gisborne – grateful thanks to showjumper Sarah Aitken and polo player Tom Lane who provided inspiration in so many ways. Lastly to my brilliant bay gelding, Ash – I couldn't have done it without you.*

www.stacygregg.co.uk

First published in Great Britain by HarperCollins *Children's Books* in 2011
HarperCollins *Children's Books* is a division of HarperCollins*Publishers* Ltd,
77-85 Fulham Palace Road, Hammersmith, London, W6 8JB

1

Text copyright © Stacy Gregg 2011

ISBN 978-0-00-733345-5

Stacy Gregg asserts the moral right to be identified
as the author of the work.

Typeset in 11.5/20pt Palatino by Palimpsest Book Production Limited,
Falkirk, Stirlingshire

Mixed Sources
Product group from well-managed
forests and other controlled sources
www.fsc.org Cert no. SW-COC-001806
© 1996 Forest Stewardship Council
FSC

FSC is a non-profit international organisation established to promote the
responsible management of the world's forests. Products carrying the FSC
label are independently certified to assure consumers that they come
from forests that are managed to meet the social, economic and
ecological needs of present and future generations.

Find out more about HarperCollins and the environment at
www.harpercollins.co.uk/green

Chapter One

When Georgie Parker packed her bags for Blainford Academy she was the talk of Little Brampton. The local girl made good, she had aced the UK auditions and earned herself a place at the exclusive international equestrian boarding school in Lexington, Kentucky, USA. Everyone in her tiny Gloucestershire village agreed that she was destined to follow in her famous mother's footsteps and take the eventing world by storm.

Now she was back for Christmas break after a term away. As she stood shivering in the snow at the gates of Lucinda Milwood's riding school, Georgie wasn't feeling quite as upbeat about her homecoming as she'd expected.

Above her head, the dark clouds promised another snowfall that evening. The yard was empty and Georgie figured the horses must be already tucked up in their loose boxes, waiting for their hard feed. She clacked open the gates to the yard and walked up the driveway, heading for the stable block.

At the front door Georgie stood for a moment, taking a deep breath, inhaling the smell of straw, horse sweat and liniment. These stables had been a second home after her mum had died. She would come here every day before and after school to help Lucinda with the ponies, grooming and mucking out in exchange for lessons on her black Connemara, Tyro.

After Georgie made it into Blainford, she had kept in touch with Lucinda, but over the past few weeks she had failed to email her old instructor. Afraid to tell Lucinda about what had happened last term, she had delayed the inevitable. But she knew she couldn't put it off any longer.

Or maybe she could. Lucinda was nowhere to be seen.

"Hello? Lucinda?" Georgie's voice echoed through

the empty stable block. She was about to turn and walk out again when the tack-room door opened and a woman with dark brown hair appeared, carrying three heavy feed buckets.

Struggling with her armful of buckets, the woman barely glanced up at the blonde girl in the corridor. "I'm sorry," she grunted, "but if you've come to enquire about signing up for lessons you'll need to come back next week. We're closed until January the fifth…"

Georgie laughed. "Lucinda! Have I really been gone so long you don't even recognise me?"

There was a moment of disbelief and then Lucinda Milwood let out a joyful shriek, dropping the feed buckets as she raced over to Georgie and enveloped her in the most enormous hug.

"Georgie!" she cried. "What on earth are you doing here? I thought you weren't arriving until tomorrow!"

"I got an early flight," Georgie grinned. "I told Dad and Lily not to say anything. I wanted to surprise you."

Lucinda beamed at her former pupil. "It's so good to see you. I swear you've grown taller than me – what are they feeding you at that school?"

"Ughhh! I do not want to even think about boarding-school food for the next few weeks!" Georgie pulled a face.

"Here," Lucinda handed her a bucket. "Help me finish off the feeds and then I'll make us a nice cup of tea and you can tell me everything about school. How are your classes?"

"Ummm... well, actually..." Georgie started to say, but Lucinda had already headed off down the corridor.

"Give your one to Dooley," she shouted back over her shoulder. "He's in the first box."

Georgie headed for the first stall and swung open the bottom half of the Dutch door, ducking underneath the top half to hang the bucket in the empty bracket on the wall.

This first loose box held a big piebald cob: black and white patches with a thick mane, fluffy feet and one blue wall eye. When he saw Georgie, the cob strode straight up to her, nickering his grateful thanks.

"Hey, Dooley." Georgie gave the piebald a firm pat on his broad neck. "How've you been?"

Georgie stepped aside and watched as the black and

white gelding shoved his muzzle deep into the bucket and began snuffling up the chaff and sugarbeet.

"He looks good, doesn't he?" Lucinda said, joining her in the loose box to admire the horse.

Georgie nodded. "He was always one of my favourites."

"I've got a couple of new horses since you were here last." Lucinda led Georgie back out into the corridor and passed her another feed bucket. "Shamrock and Jack Sparrow. Come on, I'll introduce you."

Shamrock turned out to be a rangy chestnut Thoroughbred with bony hindquarters and deep brown eyes, while Jack Sparrow was a small, fleabitten grey pony with a wilful look about him.

"They're both for the school, but Jack is proving to be a bit of a handful for most of the riders," Lucinda admitted. "He's been getting away with murder. He raced off with Davina Pike the other day and deposited her over a fence. Not that I can say that I blame him – there are many times when I've wanted to do the same thing myself!"

She smiled at Georgie. "It's so good to have you back!

The horses have missed you terribly. Dooley and Billy could both do with some schooling work if you have time."

Georgie nodded. "I'm yours for the next two weeks."

"Well I could certainly use your help," Lucinda said. "It's been impossible to find good grooms since you've been away." Lucinda put the last feed bin in the loose box and shut the door. "So, is cross-country class going OK? I hope Tara hasn't been too tough on you this term."

Tara Kelly, an old school friend of Lucinda's, was the head of the Blainford eventing department. Renowned for being the toughest teacher at the academy, Tara had been Georgie's cross-country teacher for the past term.

When Georgie had arrived at the academy she had expected to excel in Tara's class. After all, at the age of thirteen she was already the best junior cross-country rider in Gloucestershire. But things were different at Blainford. Thrust among elite, hand-picked equestrians from all over the world, she was facing real competition for the first time.

To make things even harder she had been forced to sell her beloved Tyro because she couldn't afford to take him to America and pay his boarding fees. Georgie was trying to cope with a new horse, Belladonna, a talented but headstrong mare.

Struggling to click with her new mount, Georgie found herself at the bottom of the class rankings, fighting to survive the gruelling end-of-term eliminations. Tara Kelly was known for axing students from her freshman intake if they didn't measure up to her exacting standards. Which brought Georgie to the big news that she needed to tell Lucinda.

"I've been dropped from Tara Kelly's class."

The words tumbled out of her mouth before she could stop them. Lucinda stared at her in stunned disbelief.

"Georgie! But why? I thought you said that you had Belle going really well?"

"I do... now," Georgie groaned. "Belle has been brilliant ever since the House Showjumping, but we had lots of trouble earlier in the term and then on finals day she would have been OK except Kennedy forced me off the course on the steeplechase. I had to pull Belle up or she would have got hurt."

It sounded so lame, like she was making excuses for her bad performance. But she wasn't. Her expulsion from class was unfair and it had been masterminded by Blainford's own resident evil – Kennedy Kirkwood.

"Did you tell Tara what happened?" Lucinda asked. "If this Kennedy forced you off the jump then she should be reprimanded…"

"I tried," Georgie sighed, "but Tara didn't see it – she had no choice. I'd been at the bottom of the rankings all term and so she eliminated me."

"Do you want me to talk to Tara?" Lucinda offered. "I could call her and—"

Georgie shook her head. It would only make things worse.

"I know I should just get over it and take another subject, but…" Georgie took a deep breath, "… eventing class is the whole reason I wanted to go to Blainford in the first place. I know it sounds so pathetic, Lucinda, but I just don't know what I'm going to do…"

"Oh, Georgie! Why didn't you tell me? You poor

thing." Lucinda put her arms round Georgie once more, hugging her even tighter, as the tears that Georgie had been fighting to hold back finally began to flow.

✳

Two weeks in Little Brampton was just what Georgie needed to recover from that last dreadful term at Blainford. Even if not all of her friends were as understanding as Lucinda.

"It sounds awful at your stupid boarding school – getting dumped from cross-country class! I don't understand why you want to go back!"

Georgie's best friend Lily had never been one to hide her feelings. She'd been outright miserable when Georgie had decided to leave Little Brampton and now that she saw her chance to convince Georgie to turn her back on Blainford she wasn't going to leave it alone.

"You always say that cross-country is the most important bit of eventing," Lily said, "so you might as well chuck the whole business!"

"It's not that simple," Georgie insisted. "Lucinda says

I shouldn't give up. I should try to convince Tara to let me back into her class."

"How are you going to do that?"

Georgie shook her head. "I don't know yet. And I've got to choose a new subject to take in the meantime. I think I'll do dressage…"

"I don't understand dressage," Lily sighed. "I mean, it's just riding around in circles, isn't it? It's like 'Look, everyone, I've got a horse!'"

Georgie groaned. It was impossible trying to explain riding to Lily. She was simply not horsey. Right now she was on her bike, cycling alongside Georgie who was riding Toffee, one of the horses from Lucinda's stables. Georgie had tried to convince Lily to ride one of the other ponies, but Lily wasn't having any of it.

"I'll stick with my bike, thanks – at least it doesn't bolt off or try to buck," she said firmly, strapping on her cycle helmet.

The two girls rode through the village, heading towards the shops with five pounds to spend on fish and chips.

"We'll get loads for a fiver," Lily said confidently. "Nigel is working today."

"Look at you! You've sold your love to Nigel for a piece of battered cod," Georgie teased.

Nigel Potts's parents owned the fish and chip shop, and he was constantly harassing Lily to go out with him. It seemed that his persistence had finally paid off.

"I'm not actually going out with him or anything!" Lily insisted as she cycled on. "It was just the one date. He took me to the cinema and he ponged so badly of fish and chips it was like sitting next to a deep-fat fryer."

Lily sighed. "It's hardly glamorous, is it? Not like you and your handsome polo player whisking you off for a romantic weekend in the country."

"… a romantic weekend in which he dumped me with his hideous sister, and then ran off to snog her best friend!" Georgie clarified.

Her relationship with James Kirkwood had ended super-badly – even if he and Georgie had made peace at the School Formal at the end of term.

"Well, what about Riley?" Lily asked. "You're going out with him now, right?"

"I don't know," Georgie groaned. "He turns up at the

School Formal, and everything is great, but then he does a total disappearing act on me."

That night at the School Formal when Riley had taken Georgie in his arms and assured her that they would find a way to convince Tara to take her back, she had felt so safe, certain that somehow everything would be OK again. Georgie wasn't going to let Kennedy steal her future. She would fight her way back into the cross-country class.

But that confidence had begun to ebb away. Waking up in the cold light of day the next morning she realised she had no idea how to persuade Tara to reinstate her in the cross-country class. And Riley never called.

"But you'll see him when you get back to school?" Lily said.

Georgie shook her head. "He doesn't go to Blainford. He thinks the academy is full of rich snobs."

"So let me get this straight," Lily said, peddling harder so that Georgie had to push Toffee into a trot to keep up. "You've been dumped by two boys and one teacher and you're still going back? Geez, Georgie! What's it going to take to convince you to come home?"

＊

Nigel was behind the till when the two girls arrived at the Fish Pott.

"All right then, Georgie?" Nigel greeted her. "Back from your la-di-dah school for the holidays?"

"Ignore him," Lily said, looking pointedly at Nigel. "He got dipped in batter as a child and he's never been the same since."

Nigel smiled at her. "Have you come in to make an order, Lily, or have you just come in to see me?"

"Not likely!" Lily snorted. "We'll have two fishburgers and chips, thanks."

The burgers and chips were warm tucked beneath Georgie's vest to keep them safe for the ride home.

"Is that what everyone thinks about me?" Georgie asked Lily as she mounted up again on Toffee. "That I'm some stuck-up posh girl now, just because I go to Blainford?"

"Don't listen to Nigel. He's just jealous because the furthest he's ever been in his life is Tewkesbury for the late-night shopping."

Lily sighed. "I wish you were coming home for good, though, Georgie. I really miss you."

Georgie felt a lump sticking in her throat. It was so weird being back in Little Brampton again. Her dad had been beside himself with delight and Georgie noticed that he made sure he was home early every night. On Christmas Day he'd even cooked a massive Christmas dinner and invited Lily and Lucinda over.

Lucinda had been really kind too, encouraging Georgie to try out every single horse in the stables. Georgie had great new friends at Blainford, like Alice and Emily and Daisy, but she and Lily had known each other forever.

However, even though the past term at Blainford had been tough, Georgie was dying to get back on the plane to Lexington. She loved Little Brampton – but this wasn't where she wanted to be. Blainford had given her a glimpse of the future and the rider that she could become. She was determined to become an international eventer like her mother, to travel the world and live a life full of excitement, glamour and horses – lots of horses.

"I have to go back," she told Lily. "It's not over yet."

Chapter Two

*I*t had been a white Christmas in Kentucky and when the students arrived back at Blainford Academy they found the entire school grounds covered in a deep blanket of snow.

"If we can't actually see the quad, does that mean we're allowed to walk on it?" Alice wondered as the girls headed to the dining hall. "Technically we wouldn't be touching the grass."

Blainford was a college steeped in traditions – and the square of turf in the middle of the school was deemed hallowed ground. Only prefects and schoolmasters were allowed to walk across the grass, as Georgie had found out the hard way on her first day at the academy.

Conrad Miller had caught her on the grass and given

her Fatigues – a Blainford punishment that was a cross between detention and hard labour.

Conrad was the head prefect of Burghley House. There were six boarding houses at the academy, three for girls and three for boys. Each of them was named after one of the six famous four-star eventing courses in the world.

Georgie and her friends Alice Dupree, Daisy King and Emily Tait were all boarders in Badminton House. Kennedy Kirkwood, Arden Mortimer and their toxic clique of showjumperettes were in Adelaide House. Kennedy's brother, James, was in Burghley House with the vile Conrad. Georgie's eventing friends Cameron and Alex were in Luhmuhlen.

The third girls' boarding house was Stars of Pau and many of its occupants belonged to the dressage clique. Unlike other schools where jocks and geeks ruled the cliques, at Blainford the social scene was defined by what kind of rider you were and dressage placed you firmly at the bottom of the coolness order.

The polo boys and the showjumperettes – rich, spoilt and good-looking – considered themselves to be at the top. The eventing clique wasn't as flashy or glamorous as the showjumpers and polo players, but eventers still had an aura of undeniable cool about them. After all, to ride cross-country you needed nerves of steel and unshakable courage.

The first-year eventers came from all points of the globe, and although they were very different from each other, the riders had quickly formed a tight-knit bond. Their group included Georgie Parker, and her best friend Alice Dupree, a native of Maryland, and the third sister in her family to attend the college. Georgie's friend Cameron Fraser was an eventing rider from Coldstream in the Scottish Border country. Then there was Emily Tait, a shy New Zealand girl who rode a school horse, a jet-black Thoroughbred called Barclay. Naïve and slightly nervous on the ground, Emily was a rock in the saddle and had won top placing in the mid-term exam.

Daisy King had been the only rider that Georgie actually knew before she arrived. Back in England, Daisy had been Georgie's stiffest competition on the eventing circuit. Unlike Georgie, Daisy could afford to board her own horse at Blainford. She had travelled her big, grey Irish Hunter, Village Voice, all the way from the UK.

Apart from Cameron Fraser, the other eventing boys included Shanghai-born and Oxford-raised Alex Chang and his grey gelding Tatou; over-confident Australian riding phenomenon Matt Garrett with his stunning dun gelding Tigerland; and the arrogant but extremely talented French rider, Nicholas Laurent and his horse Lagerfeld.

The eventing riders gathered together at their usual table in the dining hall for the first lunch of the new term. They were close friends, but also rivals, each of them striving to come top in the class. Class rankings were considered important in every subject, but in Tara's class they were especially crucial. Cross-country was the only class where the bottom-ranked pupil was routinely eliminated at the end of every half term.

Tara Kelly justified eliminations because of the very real danger involved with riding cross-country. If a student wasn't making the grade in her first-year class then she needed to be eliminated before getting hurt – or worse.

As they sat down to eat lunch, Emily, Cameron and Daisy were vigorously debating the new school rule that made air-tech inflatable jackets compulsory at all times on the cross-country course. At the other end of the table, Nicholas, who had just returned from Bordeaux, was raving to Matt Garrett about his brand-new Butet, a French close-contact saddle made from tan calfskin leather, insisting that it gave him superior lower leg contact.

Georgie, meanwhile, sat and picked listlessly at her lasagne. She looked up at the clock. It was almost time for the afternoon riding classes to begin. In a moment they would all be heading for the stables to tack up for their first cross-country ride of the new year. But Georgie wouldn't be joining them.

"So, you still haven't told me," Alice said, leaning forward conspiratorially across the table to her, "what option class are you taking now?"

The rest of the table suddenly went quiet. It was the question that they'd all been dying to ask Georgie, but none of them had been brave enough to broach the subject.

Georgie didn't have to answer because at that moment Mitty Janssen came over to join them.

Mitty was a dedicated dressage rider who had aced the Netherlands auditions. Her two best friends, Isabel Weiss and Spanish rider Reina Romero were also dressage fanatics and boarders in Stars of Pau. All three girls were swotty and serious and known throughout the school as the 'Dressage Set'.

"Hi, Georgie," Mitty said.

"Oh, hey, Mitty, how are you?"

"So," Mitty smiled, "I heard the news that you're joining us! Do you need to borrow a pair of Carl Hester training reins? They're compulsory for first years—"

"Uh, thanks, Mitty," Georgie said, cutting her off. "I already bought some."

"OK," Mitty said cheerfully. "Well, I'll see you in class!"

"Yeah," Georgie muttered. She didn't look up from her lunch. She could feel the eyes of the rest of the eventing clique staring at her with horror. Georgie Parker had joined the dressage class!

✳

"You've got nothing to be embarrassed about," Alice insisted as the girls walked towards the stables. "I mean, dressage is an important part of eventing. It's one of the three phases. So of course it makes sense to join the dressage class!"

"Do you really think so?" Georgie was relieved, "I thought you'd think it was—"

"Wussy?" Cameron offered.

"Totally lame?" Daisy suggested.

The eventers snorted and giggled.

"Yeah, great, guys, thanks for that. I knew I could rely on your support..." Georgie groaned. "Look, what else am I supposed to do? Dressage is something I need to learn, and besides, it fits the options timetable."

"It's a good choice," Emily said, trying to be supportive. "I mean, really we should all be taking dressage as an option. You live and die by your dressage points these days. Eventing's not just about showjumping and cross-country any more."

"Hey," Georgie said, "if you wanted to drop cross-country and join dressage too, I know that there're still a couple of spaces..."

"Are you kidding?" Emily was horrified. "Trotting in circles like a nana? I'd be bored to tears!"

Georgie knew what she meant. An eventing rider lived for the thrill of galloping across country, tackling any obstacle that presented itself. After the wild, reckless excitement of Tara's class, she was well aware that Bettina Schmidt's dressage lessons would be rather... sedate. Even so, she had to stay positive.

"Bettina is a great dressage teacher," she told the others. "It's going to be cool."

✳

"For our lesson today," Bettina Schmidt said, "we will be spending the entire hour and a half at the walk to focus on our lower leg position."

"Strangle me with a martingale and put me out of my misery," Georgie groaned. Beneath her, Belladonna shifted about restlessly. The bay mare had just spent the past two weeks being spelled for the school holidays and this was their first ride together. What Belle really needed was a decent canter to blow out the cobwebs. Instead, they were going to spend their whole lesson at the walk!

Georgie joined the back of the ride and resigned herself to her fate, but Belle wasn't so biddable. As the other dressage horses began to circle the arena, walking politely on the bit, their necks arched and their strides neat and regular, Belle began skipping about with frustration.

Despite Georgie's best efforts to calm her, the mare kept racing past the others and spent the first half of the lesson in a constant jiggly-jog.

When she finally got the mare to walk on and could concentrate on what Bettina was saying, Georgie realised that she didn't actually understand most of Bettina's instructions anyway.

"Ride from the hindquarters!" Bettina kept telling her. "Now try to feel each stride. *Volte!* Stay off the forehand!"

For all Georgie knew a *volte* might be a handstand! As it turned out, it was just a little circle. They spent the lesson doing endless little circles at the walk, and then bigger ones, also at the walk.

It was all so precise, so detailed and so... very, very boring.

"That was a brilliant lesson!" Isabel Weiss's eyes were bright with enthusiasm as they led the horses back to the stables after class. "I really noticed how deep my seat was by the end of the session, didn't you, Georgie?"

"Uh-huh," Georgie agreed, stifling a yawn.

"Do you want to come back to Stars of Pau with us after we unsaddle?" Mitty offered. "We've got a DVD that shows you how to do a piaffe in ten easy steps. We were going to watch it before dinner."

"Umm, maybe some other time," Georgie said. "I'll catch you guys later, OK?"

It was a relief to be alone again in the loose box with Belle. As Georgie unsaddled the mare she was surprised to see that she wasn't even sweating under her numnah. *Mind you*, Georgie thought, *why would Belle break a sweat when she had only been dawdling around for the past hour and a half?*

Georgie looked at her watch. It was quarter to five. It would be dark by five-thirty; she should really be untacking and heading back to the house. But she felt as if she hadn't really had a proper ride.

"Come on, Belle," she murmured to the mare, flinging

the saddle over her back again and tightening the girth once more. "Let's go – just you and me."

✳

Snow had begun falling as Georgie set out along the bridle path at the back of the stables. She watched the white flakes floating down from the sky, landing on Belle's jet-black mane. Georgie usually kept it neatly pulled so that it was short and tidy for plaiting, but over the holidays it had grown lustrous and long. Belle's hunter clip was growing out too. It had been almost a term since Georgie clipped her in grooming class.

Georgie's own hair was braided in two thick, blonde plaits and as she put on her helmet to leave the stables she came up with the genius idea of twisting her plaits and shoving the ends through the ear-hole sections at the sides of her helmet so her hair would cover and protect her ears from the cold. It looked a bit weird with her plaits poking out from her helmet at odd angles, but Georgie figured that no one was going to see her.

She rode past the snug indoor arena where they had spent their dressage lesson. It felt good to be outdoors, to feel the icy bite of the winter chill against her bare cheeks.

As soon as they were clear of the stables and had passed through the gateway where the bridle path led to the open fields, Georgie urged Belle into a trot. The mare had lovely, floaty paces and she lifted up beneath Georgie like a hovercraft, arching her neck and taking the reins forward. She snorted and pulled, keen to canter.

"Steady, girl," Georgie cautioned the mare. The track was twisty and turny, and the ice had made the surface slippery – not ideal for canter work. Georgie decided to turn off the track, riding the mare across the open pasture towards an uphill stretch that led to the woods. As soon as they reached the hill Georgie tipped up into two-point position, put her legs on and Belle responded eagerly, her legs working like dark pistons making holes in the white snow.

Belle knew the terrain here well and, even though it was covered in snow, Georgie trusted the mare to be sure-footed as they cantered on. It felt so good to have some fun instead of walking around getting in touch with your seatbones!

As they crested the top of the hill, Georgie pulled Belle back to a trot as she saw the rider up ahead of her. At a distance all that Georgie could make out was the colour of the horse – a chestnut – and the rider's jersey – ice blue, the colour of Burghley House. Knowing her luck it would be Conrad Miller, and he would find some pathetic school rule about not being allowed out in the snow and give her Fatigues.

She had just decided to turn round and give them a wide berth, when the rider on the chestnut horse waved to her.

Georgie steadied Belle and peered at the horizon. The rider on the chestnut waved once more and then urged his horse on into a canter, coming up the hill from the other side towards her. Georgie watched the way he rode, completely fearless, relying on his perfect balance to control the horse, with reins held so long they were almost at the buckle. And then she realised that she knew him.

It was James Kirkwood.

James cantered right up to her and pulled his horse to a halt. "Hi, Parker. Have a good holiday?"

Suddenly face to face with him, Georgie's first thought was her hair. The hair earmuff trick had worked – her ears were nice and toasty. But she knew that she must look ridiculous, like some sort of demented Pippi Longstocking. And here she was for the first time with the boy who had dumped her last term.

"My holidays?" Georgie said, self-consciously trying to flatten her sticky-outy plaits. "OK, I guess."

James grinned. "Don't give me too much detail, will you? We might end up having a conversation."

Georgie wanted more than anything to pull her helmet off and fix the plaits, but she was certain she would have helmet-hair underneath. Luckily James didn't seem to have noticed the weird hairdo.

"I went back home to Little Brampton," she said. "Dad cooked a massive Christmas dinner and everyone came over. Apart from that I was at Lucinda's helping out at the stables. How about you?"

"The usual Kirkwood family Christmas," James groaned. "The stepmom spent the whole time planning cocktail parties for people that she doesn't even like. Dad disappeared with the hounds every day and

Kennedy and I managed to stay in different wings of the house most of the time so we could avoid speaking to each other."

"Sounds like fun," Georgie said dryly.

"Belvedere misses you," James added, referring to the big brown hunter that Georgie had ridden when she had stayed at the Kirkwood mansion. "I took him for a hack to cheer him up and we went down to the edge of the woods – you know, where we went that day?"

He gave Georgie that cute lopsided grin of his. She knew the woods that James meant. They had been out hunting and they had somehow ended up there alone. That was when he kissed her. Georgie felt herself blush. Was James flirting with her again?

"So anyway," James tried to sound casual, "are you still seeing that guy? The one you were with at the School Formal? What's his name again?"

"Riley," Georgie said. She wasn't about to tell James that she hadn't spoken to Riley since the Formal, or that she wasn't even sure if she was still dating him.

"He doesn't go to Blainford, does he?" James asked.

"No," Georgie said, "he's at Pleasant Hill High School."

"So this Riley," James said. "How did you meet him if he doesn't go to school here?"

"He's Kenny's nephew," Georgie said. "He was helping me to school Belle."

"So, he's some kind of horse whisperer?" James sneered.

"No," Georgie said, "He rides trackwork. Racehorses."

"Does he have his own stables?"

"You're asking a lot of questions about him," Georgie frowned. "You're acting like my dad."

"Am I?" James said, a fraction too quickly. "I'm just wondering what you see in him, that's all. A guy like that…"

"Like what?" Georgie said.

"You know," James said. "He's not one of us, is he?"

"I didn't know there was an 'us'," Georgie said.

"Oh, yeah," James said. "Totally. There's a 'you', and there's a 'me' and I definitely think there's an 'us'…"

As he said this he reached out a hand and gently touched Georgie's cheek. "You've got a snowflake on you," he said. "I thought I'd better wipe it off."

Suddenly Georgie's cheeks burned so hot they could have thawed a snowdrift.

"I better get back," she somehow managed to get the sentence out. "It's getting late."

"I'll come with you," James said. "This snow is getting pretty heavy."

They walked back down the hill, both of them staying off the subject of Riley. Instead, they talked about their new classes for the term. James was a year ahead of Georgie and he was a showjumper. But he'd already decided that next year he would switch his option and major in polo.

"I tried to fight it, I guess," he said. "It was just such a cliché, what with my dad being on the school polo team when he was at Blainford. I wanted to be different, but I'm playing for Burghley this season and Heath Brompton, the polo master, thinks I could go pro one day. I guess it's in the blood, you know. Like with you and your mom and eventing."

"Not so much," Georgie groaned. "I'm out of the cross-country class this term, remember?"

"Oh, yeah," James winced. "Sorry, I wasn't thinking. What are you taking instead?"

"Dressage," Georgie said.

"And it's not going well?"

"It's so boring," Georgie said. "And everything is complicated. It's like she's speaking a foreign language."

"German?"

Georgie giggled. Bettina *was* also her German teacher.

"I'll get used to it, I suppose," Georgie said, trying to sound positive.

They had arrived at the turn-off that led to her stables.

"Well, this is me," she said. "I guess I'll see you later."

"I guess you will," James said. He turned his chestnut to ride away and then he halted the horse and looked back at her.

"By the way," he gave her that killer grin, "love the Princess Leia plaits."

✳

Georgie didn't know quite what to make of her conversation with James. He'd seemed jealous at the mention of Riley – but he was the one that had split up with her! Although, it wasn't actually James's fault that they'd broken up – it was Kennedy's meddling that had caused it.

Her heart was still thudding as she unsaddled Belle and rugged the mare up for the evening, letting her loose with her hard feed. Did James want to get back together again? And was that what she wanted too?

It must have been freezing cold as she walked back from the stable block to Badminton House, but Georgie didn't notice. She felt as if she were floating like a snowflake, light and ethereal. It was getting late and the skies were darkening. As she walked along the driveway the lights above her began flickering on. They glowed overhead, lighting her way like a row of tiny moons illuminating the road between the school and the boarding houses.

Still walking on air, Georgie bounded up the steps of Badminton House. She was about to open the door when she heard the voice behind her.

"Georgie!"

She turned round. There was a boy, his dark brown hair squashed underneath a woollen beanie. He was wearing a blue and black checked shirt and dark denim jeans. Swinging the door shut on his red pick-up truck he walked up the path and that was when Georgie saw the bunch of white flowers in his hand that were clearly intended for her.

It was Riley.

Chapter Three

"**W**elcome back," Riley said, holding out the white lilies to her.

Georgie had never been given flowers before – apart from the time her dad bought her a pot plant when she was in hospital having her tonsils out, but that didn't really count. The lilies had a deep, musky perfume. Snow was falling on the petals. They were still standing there on the doorstep and no one was saying anything.

"Hey," Riley broke the silence. "I'm sorry that I never called you after the Formal. I got really busy with the horses and—"

"I can't ask you in," Georgie blurted out. "We're not allowed to have boys in the boarding house without a permission note. Besides, I have to get changed for dinner."

They stood there for another moment or two, and then Riley raked a hand uneasily through his hair and grabbed his keys out of his coat pocket. "It's OK," he said, looking back over his shoulder at the pick-up truck. "I've gotta go anyway. I promised Uncle Kenny I'd bring the truck back straight away and I've been waiting here a while now."

He smiled at Georgie. "I just wanted to say hi, you know, and that..." he hesitated, "I've missed you while you were away."

Then he looked embarrassed. "Anyway," he began, backing down the stairs towards the truck, "I better go now."

He was halfway back down the path when Georgie called after him, "Riley, wait!"

He turned round. "Yeah?"

"Thanks for the flowers. They're really beautiful."

Riley smiled. "I'll give you a call, OK?"

He got in the pick-up, slammed the door and drove off. Georgie watched the tail-lights disappear into the dark and then went inside. The clock on the wall said six-fifteen, which meant that all the boarders would be in their rooms getting ready for dinner. The first-year boarders all lived downstairs, and each of them shared a room with one other girl. Georgie had been sharing with Alice Dupree ever since Alice took the liberty of swapping her name for Daisy King's on their first day of school.

Alice was lying on her bed when Georgie came in. She was studying a riding manual and had it open to a page about fitting martingales.

"Nice lilies," she said without looking up from her book. "Riley must have spent a fortune on them."

"How did you know they were from Riley?" Georgie asked.

"Because he's been sitting out there in that pick-up truck for the past two hours waiting for you," Alice said.

Georgie was shocked. "He's been out there all that time?"

"I took him a cup of hot chocolate about an hour ago," Alice said. "He looked really cold."

Georgie had been so shocked to have Riley just turn up on the doorstep like that, she hadn't known how to deal with him at all. He'd turned up out of the blue at the School Formal too. Didn't he know how to use a phone?

"Why are you so late, anyway?" Alice asked. "School finished ages ago. Were you having so much fun studying dressage that you couldn't drag yourself away?"

Georgie shook her head. "I went for a hack after class. And then I saw James."

Alice frowned. "You mean Riley?"

"No. I saw James first. I took Belle out on the bridle paths behind the stables and I ran into James. And we… talked."

Alice looked suspicious. "When you say that you 'talked'," she did air quotes round the word, "does that actually mean you really talked or do you mean… you know…"

Georgie's eyes went wide. "No, Alice! I have not been out on a snog-a-thon with James Kirkwood!"

"Well, what about Riley then?" Alice asked.

Georgie shook her head. "There was no kissing! We hardly even spoke. I took the flowers and then I kind of ran. It was pretty bad. I was confused."

"But you're dating Riley, right?" Alice said. "I thought everything was all on with you two after the School Formal?"

Georgie flopped face-down on the bed and groaned. "Is it? I don't know. I thought it was, but then he never even called me. I spent all the holidays wondering what was going on and thinking that maybe it was over and now he turns up with flowers."

"Don't complain. At least someone is buying you flowers," Alice replied. "I'm giving up on Cam."

"Really?" Georgie said. "I thought you guys were getting on really well."

"We do get on well," Alice said. "It's just… he doesn't think of me, you know, like *that*. I'm not some bombshell like Kennedy Kirkwood."

"That's not true," Georgie said.

"It is!" Alice insisted. "Cameron stares at her like a puppy looking at a bag of Purina. He doesn't even notice me."

"You just need to get his attention. You've got to do something to make him notice you."

There was a knock at the door and Emily stuck her head in.

"Are you guys coming to dinner or what? We've been waiting for you for ages!"

✳

When Georgie had first arrived at Blainford last September the walk to the dining hall each evening hadn't been a big deal. It had been early autumn and the stroll up the tree-lined driveway had been kind of fun.

Now winter had set in and the five hundred metres from their boarding house to the main buildings of the school seemed like an intrepid hike up the Himalayas. It was freezing cold, and the girls were bundled up in school scarves, jerseys and blazers over their winter uniform of a navy wool pinafore and long black wool tights.

"I think we should be allowed to layer our jods underneath our pinafores in winter," Alice said, teeth chattering with cold as they walked round the quad to the door of the dining hall.

"We could wear them underneath our tights," Emily suggested. "Maybe no one would notice."

When they reached the dining-room doors they were relieved to see that the queue didn't stretch all the way outside and they were able to go straight indoors where it was warm. The dining room was one of the oldest buildings in the school. Outside, it was red Georgian brick, like the other buildings that surrounded the quad. Inside, the walls were dark-wood panelled, and hung with photos of famous riders who had once attended the academy. According to the blackboard menu, tonight's dinner was 'Meatloaf a la Betty-Lou'.

Alice wrinkled up her nose. "If the menu says meatloaf then why does it smell like fish?"

Daisy King shrugged. "I suppose it's better than fish smelling like meatloaf."

The girls took their loaded trays and stood in the centre of the dining hall, waiting for Georgie to have her food dished up. At the far side of the room, sitting at their usual table, were the rest of the eventing gang

– Alex and Cameron and Matt and Nicholas. The girls began to walk over to join them when Georgie heard her name being called.

"Georgie, we're here!"

Georgie saw Isabel Weiss waving at her, beckoning her over. Isabel was sitting with Mitty and Reina.

"Come and sit with us," Isabel called out to her cheerfully.

Georgie didn't know what to do. Daisy, Alice and Emily had all stopped and were watching her.

"Georgie?" Alice said. "What's going on?"

Georgie looked at the eager faces of the Dressage Set.

"Don't be silly," Alice muttered to Georgie. "You don't have to sit with them! It doesn't make any difference if you're not in the eventing class any more. You can still sit with us."

Georgie shook her head. "I really should go and say hi," she said, gesturing towards the dressages. "I'll catch up with you guys later back at the house, OK?"

Alice looked upset. "OK, whatever."

The dressage girls moved over to make room for their newest member.

"Hi, Georgie!" Mitty grinned at her as she sat down. "Fun lesson today, huh?"

"Ummm, yeah," Georgie said, her voice tinged with sarcasm. "All that stuff with the walking? Awesome."

No one else at the table laughed and Georgie realised that Mitty was quite serious.

"It will take you a while to get used to dressage class," Isabel said. "Bettina says this is because cross-country ruins your position."

Mitty agreed. "It's true. I was only in Tara's class for one term and it's played havoc with my hands!" She looked deeply upset.

"I don't know… I think my hands are OK," Georgie protested weakly.

Reina Romero pushed her dinner tray aside decisively and looked at Georgie. "We were thinking that we should all get together for a ride after school. Maybe tomorrow?"

"That sounds great," Georgie said. "I took Belle out for a hack today – the bridle paths are a bit frozen over, but we had a good canter up the hill behind the school. Belle took these really big canter strides through the snow – it was brilliant. We could go for a ride up there?"

"No," Reina was adamant. "I do not think so. Let us meet at the arena and we can do some schooling."

"It's not that cold outside," Georgie insisted. "If you wear a puffer jacket and gloves it's fine, honest."

Reina remained stony-faced. "I only ride Alba Clemante in the arena." Alba Clemante was Reina's horse, a grey Andalusian that had been bred from extremely rare dressage bloodlines.

"Oh," Georgie was taken aback. "Well, maybe when the snow has thawed a bit we could go for a ride up into the hills one weekend."

"Georgie," Isabel said, adopting a schoolteacher-ish tone, "we don't really like to hack the horses out. They are dressage horses. Back in Germany, I only ever rode in the arena."

"You never hack out?" Georgie was amazed. "You mean you just ride around in the dressage ring the whole time?"

Mitty shrugged. "It is too risky for injuries otherwise. Even with boots on, you might damage their legs. Besides, the horses need regular schooling."

"Horses get bored in the arena," Georgie countered.

"They need a break from their work – just like we do."

"Dressage horses need discipline," Reina said flatly.

"And I need a fruit juice," Georgie sighed, admitting defeat and getting up from the table. "Does anyone else want one?"

Georgie sat back down with her juice and zoned out the conversation around her. She stared over at the eventing table where it looked like Cameron had constructed a puissance course on his dinner plate, building a wall out of mashed potato and carrot sticks, which Alex was pretending to jump with a bread roll while Emily, Daisy and Alice cheered him on.

"Georgie?" Reina's voice jolted her back to reality and she realised that the girls were standing up with their dinner trays, waiting for her so that they could leave. She stood and picked up her tray.

"So shall we meet at the arena for that ride tomorrow after school?" Isabel said.

"Umm," Georgie hesitated, "I just remembered I have a thing… to do tomorrow after school. Maybe some other time?"

✶

The teachers' staff room was in the main building of the college, just above the Great Hall. It was the end of the day and the room was filled with the sound of cups and saucers jingling as teachers gathered for afternoon tea. Georgie stood anxiously in the doorway, peering in. Eventually her loitering caught the attention of the school bursar, Mrs Dubois, who put down her teacup and came over to see what she was up to.

Mrs Dubois was a Lexington native. She had a swept-back bouffant of blue-grey hair and wore a lilac suit with a matching frill-fronted blouse.

"Is there something I can help you with, Miss Parker?" she asked.

"I'm looking for Tara Kelly," Georgie replied.

"She's not here," Mrs Dubois said. Then she saw the pained expression on Georgie's face. "Is there something I can help you with?"

"I want to talk to her about changing classes," Georgie said.

Mrs Dubois frowned. "You've only just changed classes, Miss Parker."

"I know," Georgie said. "I want to change back. I want to be in the cross-country class again."

Mrs Dubois' brow furrowed deeper. "I doubt very much that Tara will change her mind, but you'll find her down at the stables."

Georgie knew that Mrs Dubois was right. There was no reason why Tara would take her back. But she couldn't bear another day of walking around feeling like a loser in Bettina Schmidt's dressage lessons. She had to try and get Tara to change her mind.

She found Tara in the tack room, fastidiously checking the girth straps and the stirrup leathers on the cross-country saddles.

"Unbelievable!" Tara said, holding up a pair of brown stirrup leathers that she had just taken off a flat-seat saddle on the rack in front of her. "Look at these! The stitching is frayed! It's so dangerous. Imagine riding at top speed on the course and that last stitch suddenly gives way! Deadly!"

She put the leathers aside and turned her attention to her former pupil.

"How are you, Georgie? Did you have a good Christmas break in Little Brampton?"

Georgie nodded. "It snowed a lot, but I managed to get some riding in with Lucinda."

"I hope you gave her my regards," Tara said.

Tara Kelly and Lucinda Milwood had been at school together at Blainford, along with Georgie's mother, Ginny. Maybe it was because of her nostalgia for her own school days that Tara seemed to take a special interest in Georgie. It was Tara who had made sure that Georgie was assigned Belle, and she had worked hard to help Georgie to master the difficult but talented bay mare. Not that Tara played favourites – she made that clear when she eliminated Georgie last term.

"Lucinda was a bit shocked when I told her that I was dropped from class," Georgie said.

Tara looked serious. "I know that was hard for you, Georgie. I know how much cross-country meant to you…"

"How much it *means* to me," Georgie corrected her. She was surprised at her own boldness, but there was no going back now. "Tara, I would accept it if I deserved to be kicked out, but really it wasn't my fault when Belle refused on the course." Georgie bit her lip, her voice trembling. "So I was hoping you might reconsider your decision and let me back into the eventing class."

Tara fell silent for a moment, stunned by the request.

"Georgie," she said at last, "perhaps you were unfairly dealt with in that final assessment last term. But you had been failing in my class for some time before that."

"I know Belle and I had problems," Georgie said, "but we sorted them out. She's going brilliantly now. If you just let us back in you'll see."

"I can't make exceptions for you, Georgie," said Tara, shaking her head. "How would that look to the other riders?"

"Like you cared," Georgie said. She knew she was overstepping the mark, and she expected Tara to lose her temper, but her former instructor looked sympathetic.

"I do care, Georgie. But I can't let you back into the class just like that."

Georgie nodded mutely, her heart broken. She turned and was about to leave when Tara spoke again.

"Come back and talk to me about it at the end of

term, Georgie. I may have a couple of spaces opening up in the class by then. If you're excelling in your subjects maybe then we can talk to the headmistress about your possible reinstatement."

"So you'd take me back next term?"

"You'd need to convince Mrs Dickins-Thomson. I'm not making any promises," Tara said. "Do your best for the rest of the term and then... we'll see."

✳

It was cold outside as she left the stables and Georgie was glad that she'd worn her new coat. The classic army-green Barbour her dad had given her as a Christmas gift was her prized possession.

She couldn't believe her father would know enough to buy her the jacket. Her dad had a very bad track record at choosing her presents so it must have been Lucinda's choice. Either way, Georgie didn't care – she'd loved the look on her dad's face when she had said with absolute honesty, "Thank you, Dad – it's exactly what I wanted!"

As she headed along the driveway back to Badminton

House, Georgie shoved her hands deep in the tartan-lined pockets of the Barbour. Her conversation with Tara had given her the smallest scrap of hope, but in a way that only made it worse. She would spend the whole term struggling with a new class – and for what? Tara might never take her back. What if the headmistress, Mrs Dickins-Thomson, vetoed her request? Maybe Lily was right. Why was she torturing herself like this? Tara had made it clear that she wasn't promising anything – even at the end of term. And what was she going to do in the meantime? Dressage class was a joke and—

"Parker!"

Georgie groaned. She turned round to confront the two people she had been trying to avoid ever since she arrived back at Blainford: Conrad Miller and Kennedy Kirkwood.

If Georgie had thought that the concept of Conrad and Kennedy as boyfriend and girlfriend was creepy, the actual sight of them holding hands on the driveway was even more disturbing.

Both of them were wearing standard uniform navy wool blazers and scarves. Conrad, being a senior, wore long black boots. He also wore spurs, which denoted his status as a prefect.

"Hey, Parker!" Conrad called again. "Nice jacket."

Georgie didn't respond. Conrad hadn't called out to her to give her a compliment. There was something else coming and she knew it.

"But it's not regulation school uniform," Conrad added. "Take it off now."

The look of smugness on Kennedy's face as her boyfriend gave the order was unbearable. Georgie scowled back at them.

"Don't be a numnah, Conrad. I've had a tough day, I'm freezing cold and I'm going back to my dorm, OK? Just leave me alone."

"I'm serious, Parker," Conrad said, clearly loving the thrill that his prefect powers were giving him. "That jacket isn't regulation. Take it off right now."

Bristling with anger, Georgie did as he said, pulling the coat off.

"All right. Satisfied?" She was about to turn round and leave when Conrad spoke again.

"Parker."

"What?"

"Give me the coat."

Georgie couldn't believe it. "I've taken it off, Conrad, I won't wear it at school again."

Conrad shook his head. "Not good enough. I'm confiscating it."

He stepped forward to take the coat out of Georgie's hands. For a moment she tightened her grip, but then realised that this was going to end badly for her, no matter what.

Conrad smiled as he snatched it from her and then left her with four spiteful little words. "Parker – you're on Fatigues."

Chapter Four

*I*t wasn't the fact that Conrad Miller had given her Fatigues that upset Georgie. The war between Georgie and Burghley House's head prefect meant that it was almost a Blainford tradition for Conrad to dish out punishment to her at any opportunity.

What really irked her was the jacket.

"He only confiscated my Barbour so he could give it to Kennedy," Georgie told Alice. "She's probably wearing it right now."

"I always wondered what Kennedy saw in Conrad," Alice said. "Now I realise she's in it for the power trip. He has the ability to seize Barbour."

The two girls were on their way to the stables to

saddle up for their afternoon lessons and Georgie had some big news.

"I've dropped out of dressage."

Alice was wide-eyed. "But, Georgie, you've only had one lesson!"

Georgie shrugged. "There's no point in kidding myself. I knew straight away that I didn't fit in. It was all so uptight. No one seemed to know how to have fun."

Georgie knew that she needed to find another sport that got her adrenalin surging in the way cross-country did. And when she looked through her list of options, one leapt out at her. She was taking her first Rodeo lesson today.

"Georgie Parker?"

"Yes, Mr Shepard!"

"Call me Shep," the head of the Western department said affably, pushing back the brim of his ten-gallon hat to reveal a weather-beaten face.

"Georgie, it says here that you've transferred out of dressage class?"

"Yes, Mr Shepard," Georgie said. "Well, kind of. I was

only in it for a day. Before that I was in Tara Kelly's cross-country class."

"Have you ever done any rodeo riding before?"

"No, sir, I mean Shep," Georgie corrected herself. "Apart from cattle roping in your Western class in the first term."

Shep raised a grey bushy eyebrow. "We'll give you a try in the bronc chute and see how you go," he said in his languid drawl.

Georgie followed Shep over to the round pen where his first-year Rodeo class were perched on the railings waiting for their teacher. In the bucking chute beside the round pen an unbroken stallion thrashed like a great white shark.

Shep paid no mind to the stallion crashing and banging alongside him as he addressed the class.

"We've got a new girl joining us today from dressage." He drew the last word out as he said it – 'drey-ssage'.

"This is Georgie Parker."

Georgie waved to the other riders sitting up on the railings. She recognised a few faces from her other classes. She knew Bunny Redpath and Blair Danner, and the two boys that they always hung out with – Tyler McGuane and Jenner Philips.

"Georgie, why don't you take the first ride today," Shep said. "You step on up here next to me on the platform."

Georgie sidled along the railings to the platform above the bucking chute. From here she could see the black stallion right below her. He quivered with barely suppressed terror as he stood trapped inside the railings of the tiny space. All his instincts were screaming at him to run, to escape. But instead he was forced to stand there, with the surcingle round his belly irritating him, and the girl hovered above him on the platform, making him even more nervous.

"Crouch down low," Shep told her, "and swing one leg out over to the other side of the chute like you're doing the splits right over his back."

Georgie went to do as Shep had told her, and then flinched as the stallion suddenly surged forward and slammed his chest straight against the barriers. Reeling back, the black horse pushed up on his hocks, trying to rear and Georgie felt her stomach lurch in fear as the wranglers on either side of the chute quickly sprang into action and grappled with ropes on either side to keep the stallion's head down.

"It's OK," Shep insisted, "he can't get loose. You can climb onboard."

Georgie felt her legs turn to jelly as she did the splits over the chute. She didn't know who was more terrified – her or the black horse beneath her. She wanted to pull out of this whole thing right now. But all the other riders in the rodeo class were watching her take her turn. There was no way she could back out without looking like a coward.

Still hanging on to the railing with one hand, she slowly lowered herself down into the chute, straddling the horse and gently putting her weight on his back.

As soon as the black horse felt her sitting astride him he surged forward in a wild panic, but there was nowhere for him to go. The chute was still shut tight in front of him.

"Just sit tight," Hank Shepard reassured Georgie as one of the wranglers took a tight hold of the stallion's halter. "We're nearly ready."

Shep did a last-minute check of the rigging, making sure that Georgie had her hand in the right position with the rope wrapped round and clasped in her palm. "The rope is your safety back-up in case you lose your grip," Shep explained. "When you get thrown, remember to open your hand. That way you won't get dragged."

Georgie didn't like the way Shep talked about being thrown *as if it was something that was certain to happen*. She'd spent most of her life until now trying to avoid falling. But falling off seemed to be the whole point of this sport!

"OK." Shep seemed satisfied. "Remember, hang on with your right hand and keep your left hand up in the air for balance. The chute is gonna open in just a moment and this horse here, he'll come flyin' out with his head between his legs ready to throw-in his first buck. Remember to lean back and go with him and you'll be fine."

"Ready?" Shep asked.

Georgie gave him a quick nod and suddenly the chute opened. The black horse flung himself forward and gave the most almighty buck that Georgie had ever felt in her entire life. Jacking himself up so that all four legs came off the ground at once, the black horse began to throw one buck after the other.

"Lean back!" Georgie heard Hank Shepard shout out.

She felt the stallion beneath her execute a full body twist in mid-air and the next thing she knew the soil was rushing up to meet her face.

"Stand up!" Hank Shepard was shouting at her. "Get to the rails!"

Realising the danger she was in lying there on the ground, Georgie rolled over to keep out of the way of the stallion's lethal hooves as he slammed his forelegs down into the dirt right beside her.

She stumbled to her feet, her heart racing as she ran to the side of the arena where she could climb the railing to safety.

Still shaking with the shock of the fall, she looked up at the clock on the wall above the bucking chute. Her heart sank. One point five seconds!

She had lasted on the stallion's back for less than two lousy seconds.

"Not bad for a first-timer," Shep said. He turned to the next pupil in line. "You're up, Tyler."

Tyler McGuane was a good-looking boy with lean legs, honey-tanned skin and sun-bleached blonde hair that constantly fell over his eyes. He stood above the bucking chute, chewing his gum and pulled a red bandana out of his pocket, tying it round his forehead to keep his fringe back. Then he lowered himself down on to the back of the next bareback bronc that had been lined up ready in the chute – a solid chestnut stallion by the name of Widowmaker.

Shep waited until Tyler gave him the nod and then the chute swung open with a loud bang. Widowmaker came barrelling out at top speed and flung his head down between his forelegs to start bucking. Tyler instinctively threw his torso so far back he was almost lying flat against the stallion's rump to absorb the motion. Widowmaker lashed both hind legs out towards the sky. He was bucking as hard as he could and no sooner did his hooves touch the ground than he let rip again, spinning left and right as he did so, trying to dislodge the rider on his back. Tyler was rocking back and forth, one hand waving high over his head for balance, his backside glued to the saddle.

The clock positioned above the chute was counting down the seconds. For a bareback bronc rider to win they had to last ten seconds on the bronc's back. Tyler had already reached eight seconds. Georgie watched the clock as it reached nine seconds, then ten and the bell rang. Tyler had made it!

At the far end of the arena the gates suddenly swung wide open and Tyler's best friend, Jenner Philips, galloped in on a stocky grey Quarter Horse. In a few quick strides Jenner had lined his grey horse up alongside Tyler's bronc. As Jenner pulled alongside him Tyler reached up his free arm and swung it round Jenner's shoulders. Jenner suddenly slowed the grey horse up and as the chestnut bronc kept galloping forward the two horses parted company. Tyler was yanked free and clear off Widowmaker's back so that he was dangling off the side of Jenner's grey Quarter Horse. A few strides later, Jenner had lowered his friend to the ground and Tyler, nimble as a cat, landed on his feet in the middle of the arena.

It was a faultless dismount. On the sidelines the rest of the Western class applauded and wolf-whistled to show their approval. "Way to go, Tyler!" Bunny Redpath hollered out as Tyler loped out of the arena.

In the chute Blair Danner was preparing to ride. Georgie watched her wrap her hand tight in the rigging rope, her blonde hair tied back in a ponytail and a tense expression on her pretty face.

"Now this oughta be good."

Georgie turned round. It was Tyler McGuane. He was leaning up on the railing right beside her.

"They don't come much better than Blair," Tyler said. "She's ridden bareback and saddle bronc classes at Calgary."

"Calgary?" Georgie said. "What's that?"

"Are you kiddin' me?" Tyler gave her a funny look. "The Calgary Stampede's only the biggest rodeo in the world."

Georgie shook her head. "Sorry. I'm more into English riding."

"So why have you taken up this class?" Tyler asked suspiciously. "Are you a buckle bunny or something?"

"A what?"

"*Buckle bunny*," Tyler said. "That's what cowboys call the girls who hang around the rodeo circuit."

Tyler lifted up his school shirt and at first Georgie thought he was just showing off the bull horn scars on his tanned, muscular torso, but then she realised she was meant to be looking at the buckle of his belt. It was made of bronze and imprinted with a steer head.

"I won this buckle at Calgary," Tyler lowered his shirt again.

"That's pretty cool," Georgie said.

Tyler shrugged. "It's a steer-roping buckle. The really good cowboys win their buckles for bareback or saddle bronc. The buckle bunnies all want to date a cowboy with a bronc buckle."

"You're kidding!" Georgie giggled. "You mean there are girls who honestly care about what sort of buckle you've got? Like rodeo groupies?"

"Totally," Tyler said.

"Well, no," Georgie said, more amused than insulted by the question, "I'm not a bunny."

"Then what are you doin' here?" Tyler said. "No offence, but you don't strike me as a rodeo rider."

"I got eliminated from cross-country and I needed a new option class," Georgie said.

She would never have admitted it to Tyler, but she'd picked rodeo because it looked like fun – plus it seemed like an easy subject to ace an 'A' in the exams and impress Tara. Honestly, how hard could it be to ride like a cowboy? They just seemed to flap their arms and legs to make their horses go – as far as Georgie had thought, there was no real skill involved!

Now, as she watched Blair Danner come flying out of the chute on her bronc, hanging on like she was riding a tornado, Georgie realised she was just as much out of her element here as she had been in the dressage class. She could see the concentration in Blair's eyes as she threw herself backwards with the movement of the bronc and the strength in her skinny, tanned arms as she gripped the rigging to keep her seat. As the clock ticked on towards the ten-second bell, Georgie marvelled at Blair's skill. Even while the bronc was trying to buck her off, Blair Danner was still lazily chewing her gum.

Georgie jumped down off the railing of the round pen. "I'll catch you later, OK, Tyler?"

Tyler frowned. "You're going? But class isn't over. Don't you want another turn in the chute?"

"No, thanks," Georgie smiled. "I think one humiliating fall per day is my limit."

As Georgie walked back towards the stables, she knew that she was never going back. After her epic fail in the arena she doubted that Shep would be too heartbroken to lose her, but Mrs Dubois might be a different matter. She could only imagine the look on the school bursar's face when she broke the news that she would be changing classes yet again this term. This was starting to get embarrassing.

✳

"On the plus side, at least you're sitting with us in the dining hall again," Alice pointed out when Georgie joined the eventers' table. "I could never really imagine you hanging out with the Westerns – line-dancing and Stetson-wearing is so not your thing."

"I don't know," Daisy King said, "I always thought

Georgie would suit those white leather boots with the tassels."

Georgie got up from the table and picked up her tray. "I have to go."

Daisy's face dropped. "Hey, Georgie, I was only joking…"

"I know," Georgie said. "I have to go and report to the library. Conrad Miller has put me on Fatigues, remember?"

The prefects at Blainford were ruthless, dishing out Fatigues each week and it didn't matter how trivial or huge the crime had been, everyone got the same punishment – and this week that involved cleaning the library.

"Right!" Mr Wainwright the librarian addressed the group of twelve pupils. "The sooner we get started the sooner we'll get this done. It's quite simple. Take all the books off the shelf, then using the damp cloths you've been provided with, give the shelf a good dust before putting the books back again."

The students groaned. Mr Wainwright pointed to the sign above his head that said 'Silence'.

"I'll also need some volunteers to help me sort out the archive section."

No one put their hand up.

"I'll do it, sir," Georgie offered.

"Excellent!" Mr Wainwright said. "Parker, come with me. The rest of you get dusting."

The archive room was a small windowless space at the back of the main library. The shelves were filled with rows of bound volumes.

"This is where we keep student records, school information and rare books," Mr Wainwright explained, pulling a book off the shelf and blowing the dust off the cover before he opened it up.

"These are the Blainford yearbooks," he said. "They date back almost eighty years to when the academy first opened its doors."

Mr Wainwright looked up at the shelves. "These books record our school's history – and those records would all be lost if anything happened to the library."

He plonked the heavy volume he had been holding into Georgie's hands.

"Which is why I am assigning you the task of

digitising it. I need these books scanned for storage."

"All of them?" Georgie squeaked.

"Oh, there's no way you'll get through more than a few volumes today," Mr Wainwright said. "If you got Fatigues every week for the rest of the year then you could finish the job!"

He smiled at Georgie. "That's a joke, Parker."

"Very funny, sir," Georgie said. Wainwright didn't realise that at the rate she was going with Conrad she would single-handedly have the whole library on a hard drive in no time.

Digitising the archives sounded complicated, but in fact it was really just a matter of turning the pages of the book one at a time and scanning each side as you went. In half an hour Georgie had worked her way through the first volume of the Blainford yearbook from 1930-1940. She was about to attack the next volume from 1940-1950 when she thought better of it and pushed the book back on to the shelf. It didn't matter what order she scanned the books in – so why not choose the era that actually interested her? Her eyes skimmed the spines of the volumes until she found the yearbook from

1980-1990. She opened the book and skipped forward to 1986 – the year that her mother had been a senior at the school. She scanned the student list, looking under 'P' for Parker and then suddenly realised that her mother would have been called by her maiden name, Ginny Lang.

Georgie flipped the pages back and the name leapt out at her: *Virginia Lang*. There were pictures of riders and stories of triumphs and trophies, and then she saw her own face staring back at her from the pages. Well, it had looked like her face at first. Her mother was sitting astride a grey mare, smiling for the camera, flanked by two other riders. Georgie instantly recognised them – Lucinda Milwood and Tara Kelly. The image was captioned: *Senior Eventing Class.*

Georgie flicked through the next few pages. There were pictures of pupils showjumping, a spread about the scurry racing squad and the dressage team. Suddenly there was a picture that made Georgie stop and look again. It was a brilliant action shot of the Blainford polo team. The four players were haring down the field and the player in the lead was riding at full gallop, hanging out of the saddle like an acrobat, leaning low over one knee about to take a swing at the ball with her mallet. The player was wearing a polo helmet, but even so, Georgie recognised the face immediately.

It was her mother.

Chapter Five

*G*eorgie straightened up nervously on Belle's back. She had tacked the mare up that afternoon in her cross-country gear, thinking that it was the most appropriate equipment that she had. She was wearing her whitest jodhpurs, and her long black boots along with her house colours – the red shirt of Badminton House. But as she lined up alongside the other riders, she was acutely aware that she didn't fit in. It wasn't just that the rest of the riders in this class were tacked up with their full polo kit of standing martingales, gag bits and double reins. It was also the fact that in this line-up of a dozen riders, Georgie Parker was the one and only girl.

"We have a new pupil with us today," polo master Heath Brompton told the class. He looked down at the piece of paper in his hands and then did a double take when he saw Georgie. "George Parker?"

"Georgie," she corrected him. "It's short for Georgina."

Heath Brompton looked anxious. "I must have read it wrong when I approved your transfer…" He paused. "The thing is, Parker, you're the only girl in the class."

Georgie smiled. "I can see that, sir."

Heath Brompton frowned. He didn't want a girl in his class. He'd have to make special allowances. There was only one changing room for starters; where would she get dressed? And how would she handle rough-housing with the lads? She would probably burst into tears the minute another player came near her.

"I'll have to talk to the headmistress about this," Heath harrumphed. "I doubt she'll allow—"

"Mrs Dickins-Thomson has already approved the transfer."

Heath Brompton wasn't convinced. "I'm sure the Blainford rules don't allow girls to play."

"There's nothing about girls playing polo in the school rules – I already checked."

Heath Brompton was an odd-looking man. He

reminded Georgie a little bit of Gordon Ramsay with his deep frown lines and his cheeks marked with pocks and crevices. On top of his head he had a thick thatch of black hair, and a pair of bushy black eyebrows sat heavily over his hooded eyes. He raised one of those furry brows at Georgie's comment. "It may not be in the rules as such, Parker, but I think you'll find that historically girls have never played—"

"Excuse me, sir, but my mother played for the school," Georgie insisted. Then she added with particular emphasis, "Polo is a big tradition in my family."

Georgie knew what the teachers were like here at Blainford, always on about the school traditions and customs. Well, if they wanted to play it that way then she could too. If a woman had played back in her mum's day then surely Georgie could join the team too?

When Georgie had stumbled upon her mother's photo in the yearbook it had been the first time she had ever considered polo as a possibility. She had smuggled the book back to the dorm with her and shown it to Alice.

"She was team captain," Georgie told her proudly, reading out the text beneath the picture.

"After being undefeated all season the Blainford Polo Team, led by Virginia Lang, lost their final game against Byerley Park by a narrow margin in the penalty shoot-out, with a score of eight goals to nine."

"That's your mum?" Alice had been impressed. "I thought I knew everything about this place, but I had no idea that girls used to play polo."

Neither did Georgie. She had never even considered it when she was looking for something to replace cross-country class as an option subject. She'd watched the matches at the school between the boys' houses – particularly Luhmuhlen and Burghley who held an annual grudge match at the start of the first term. Alex and Cam both played for Luhmuhlen, and James Kirkwood and Conrad both played for Burghley. But it had never occurred to Georgie that a girl could play until she saw that picture of her mum.

"This isn't going to work out, Parker." Heath Brompton looked distinctly unhappy. "You don't have the right kit. And if this is the mare you're planning to ride then she's too large. A polo mare should usually be no more than fifteen-two."

"I know she's a bit big," Georgie said, "but I've been reading about the sport and apparently a lot of the Argentinian riders are choosing taller mares now. The main thing is that the polo mare should be athletic, short-coupled with strong hocks and rump and a long neck – so she's got the perfect conformation." Georgie paused for breath. "I've already ordered my polo kit from the school store. I'll have it in time for the next lesson; this is just what I'm wearing today."

Heath Brompton didn't look any more pleased after the explanation, but it was clear this girl wasn't giving up.

"We're having stick-and-ball today," he said, reaching into his kit bag to pass Georgie a mallet. "The easiest way to learn is to just join in with the other players. You'll pick it up as you go."

Stick-and-ball turned out to be the polo equivalent of a football kick-about. There were no real rules and the point of the exercise was to settle the ponies and get them accustomed to having the mallet swung about right beside them without shying. At the same time the riders also worked on their own stick skills, practising their forehand and backhand shots.

Determined not to waste any of his precious coaching time on his new pupil, Heath Brompton promptly turned his back on Georgie and focused his energies on his best players. He shouted out advice as the riders loped about, rising up and down in the saddle with each canter stride in that peculiar way that only polo players do.

Georgie began to imitate the other riders, practising her rising canter, going up and down on the sidelines of the field.

There were several balls scattered across the fields and the riders were taking it in turns to hit them, timing it right to strike the surface cleanly with their mallets, then urging their ponies on to give chase and hit the ball a second time to pass it to the next player.

Georgie rode Belle forward to join in, but on her first attempt, she hit the ball at a skewed angle so that it bounced straight into a snowdrift on the side of the field.

"Oops!"

Heath Brompton glared at her. "Not into the snow, Parker! Down the field!"

Georgie began to try and dig the ball out with her mallet when a rider on a bay mare came over to help her.

"It's not your fault," the boy on the bay said as he used his mallet to help her dig. "We usually have the sideboards round the fields to keep the balls in, but the grounds have only just been snow-ploughed so the boards haven't been put back yet."

The boy looked at Georgie. "I know you, don't I? You're friends with Cameron Fraser and Alex Chang?"

Georgie nodded. "I used to be in their eventing class. How do you know Cam and Alex?"

"We're on the Luhmuhlen house polo team together," the boy said.

Georgie recognised him now. She had seen him playing last term against Burghley House.

The boy put his mallet in his left hand along with the bundle of reins that he was already clutching, so that he could reach over and shake her hand.

"My name is JP. JP Lewis."

"Georgie Parker," she smiled back. "Or George, according to Mr Brompton."

"So you've never played polo before?" JP asked.

"Nope."

"Would you like me to show you how to hold your stick properly?" he offered. "You've got it almost like a baseball bat the way you're holding it at the moment. It needs to be more like a golf club. Wrap the cord like this round your thumb and then the stick rests in the palm of your hand like this."

He demonstrated with his own stick, and Georgie mirrored him.

"Don't grip it tight," JP advised. "Hold it nice and loose. When you hit the ball, you don't try and whack it – keep your shoulder loose and the power comes from the timing of your swing. Here, watch me!"

JP cantered his mare out on to the field and turned back to take aim at a ball lying on the ground in front of him. He took his swing as if he had all the time in the world, shoulders loose and wrists relaxed. The mallet contacted the ball with a hard thwack and drove it all the way to the far end of the field.

"See?" JP grinned at her. "Now you have a go."

It took Georgie a few more goes to master the polo

grip and get her timing right before she could do a half-decent forehand shot. The backhand still seemed clumsy to her and she was doing something funny with her wrist. "Don't turn your mallet, just swing backwards!" JP instructed her. "That's better!"

If Georgie was taking a while to catch on, it took Belle no time at all. Right from the start, the bay mare seemed to have a natural instinct for the sport, chasing the ball down, and never flinching as Georgie swung the mallet beside her.

"She's a nice mare," JP said. "Some of them take to it straight away. They have that competitive urge to beat the other mares to the ball."

"Why are polo ponies always mares?" Georgie asked.

JP shrugged. "Mares just seem to be more aggressive than geldings on the field – they chase the ball better. Nobody knows why."

Belle stood out from the other mares on the field. Even though they were called polo ponies, they were actually horses – most of them between fifteen and fifteen-two hands high. At sixteen hands, Belle was a good two inches taller than most, which meant that

Georgie had to stretch down lower, hanging right out of the saddle to sweep at the ball. And while the rest of the ponies on the field had their tails tied up and their manes hogged to a short bristle along the neckline, Belle's mane and tail were still flowing free.

"Polo mares always have their manes hogged," JP told her. "Your hands could get tangled – plus you've already got two sets of reins and a mallet to hold. You can't have the mane getting in the way as well."

The polo mares all wore their tails tied up for the same reason. "It can really hurt a mare if she gets her tail hooked and yanked by a mallet," JP winced. He turned his mare Tosca round to show Georgie her tail.

"For stick-and-ball training, I just tie it up in an Argie knot," JP said. "But if it's like a proper tournament then I tape her tail."

"Why is it called an Argie knot?" Georgie asked.

"It's short for Argentinian Knot," JP said. "I've played a bit of polo over there – it's a much faster game than in Britain and—"

"JP!" Heath Brompton was striding across the field towards them.

"You're not going to make the squad if you spend all your time helping beginners to learn the game. Get out on the field. We've still got another ten minutes before class finishes."

Georgie followed JP out on to the field, aware that Heath Brompton was glaring at her. She focused on the ball and tried to swing at it, but nerves got the better of her and she missed the ball entirely.

"Come on, Georgie!" Heath Brompton called out, "Hit it!"

When she failed to stop the next ball and it went whistling past and smacked into the fetlocks of another pony he just about went berserk. "You're supposed to trap it! Turn that mare round! You're moving too slow. If you can't execute a turn at the canter then you're useless in a game!"

Georgie nodded to acknowledge her teacher and then rode Belle on hard after the ball. She caught up with a boy on a grey mare, and managed to put some of JP's advice into practice, stealing the ball by executing a clever sideways shot that went straight under Belle's own belly.

It was a slick move, but Heath Brompton remained unimpressed.

"A lucky shot. Your ball skills are minimal," he told Georgie as the players headed back to the changing rooms. "I can tell that you've never played before. If you're planning to remain in this class then you need to work on stick-and-ball outside of school time. We'll be dividing into teams for a game next week. I want you in proper kit. Full polo whites, gag and martingale."

At least Heath Brompton was talking about the next lesson. She hadn't actually been kicked out of his class yet.

"Oh, and Parker?" the polo master added as they rode off back towards the stables. "Get that mare's mane hogged!"

✳

The next day after school Georgie stood beside Belle with the mane clippers in her hands. She could feel the engine vibrating, ready to power the blades into action. Belle was standing there perfectly calm, unperturbed by the whirr of the motor. All Georgie needed to do was hold the clippers up against the crest of the mare's neck and run the blades along to shave the mane off at the roots from the withers to the forelock.

Georgie raised the clippers… and then completely lost her bottle, switched them off and put them down.

"I can't do it," Georgie murmured to the mare as she reached out and ran her fingers through the long, silky black strands. Belle had a gorgeous mane. It was thick and jet-black, a perfect contrast against the mare's russet-bay body. Georgie always kept it neatly pulled, so that it finished in a tidy line along the neck rather than having scraggy split ends. She imagined Belle without her mane, just the stubble left over like the bristles of a loo brush running up the crest of her neck. Ughh! It was too horrible. Georgie would rather shave her own head than do this!

She put the clippers away. There had to be some other way. She got out her grooming kit and rummaged around until she found the mane comb, glycerine gel and a packet of rubber bands. She would plait Belle up instead.

It took her an hour to plait up and by then Georgie was due on the polo field. She had arranged to meet

JP, along with Alex and Cam for a bit of casual stick-and-ball. The three boys were already there ahead of her. JP was mounted up on the same polo mare he'd ridden in class the day before, and Alex and Cam both rode two of the Luhmuhlen House polo ponies.

"Hey, Georgie," Cam smiled as she approached them. "I never picked you for a polo player." Cam tapped the ball towards her, as if he was batting a Ping-Pong ball to a kitten and Georgie responded by kicking Belle into a canter and striking the ball straight back with a fairly good forehand shot.

"Whoa!"

"Nice stroke," JP grinned. "Come on, let's play two aside. Georgie is on my team."

It was a fast-paced stick-and-ball session. This time, instead of feeling like she was totally uncoordinated, Georgie was able to hold her own against the others. By the end of the session she could strike the ball forehand and backhand and even lift her stick over Belle's shoulder to take a nearside shot.

She held the mallet in her right hand just as JP had shown her. In her other hand she now held four reins because Belle was kitted out in her new polo double bridle. Alex had explained how to hold the two sets of reins all in the one hand in the complicated arrangement known as an English Bridge. But Georgie far preferred the hold that Cameron showed her, with the reins snaking up between her fingers and thumb of her left hand, a style known as the Argentinian grip.

The practice session lasted for half an hour and by the end the ponies were sweating, flanks heaving.

JP looked over at Belle, who had worked up a lather of white foam on her neck. "So what are your other ponies like?" he asked Georgie.

"What do you mean?" Georgie asked. "I don't have any other ponies."

"Well you'll need a string," JP said. "If you're serious about playing."

"Uhh, when you say a 'string'," Georgie said anxiously, "how many ponies do you mean exactly? Like two or three?"

"Yeah, right," JP said. "Try six or seven!"

Georgie felt her heart sink. Of course she needed more

than one pony! When she thought back to the polo matches she'd seen at Blainford she'd watched them swap over ponies after each chukka. The galloping pace of a polo game was so fast and furious the ponies were exhausted after seven minutes. A fresh pony was required for each chukka – and there were six chukkas in a game!

"Don't freak out," JP said. "You can maybe get away with four ponies at low goal level – there're only four chukkas in a low goal game."

Georgie still felt sick. Four ponies were three more than she had!

Georgie looked over at Cam and Alex. "But you guys don't have your own string."

"That's true," Cam said, "but we've got the Luhmuhlen ponies to use."

Luhmuhlen and the other boys' boarding houses all had strings of sixteen school ponies in their stables, enough horses to supply a team of four boys. But the girls' boarding houses didn't have their own polo strings.

"You don't need four ponies for Heath Brompton's classes," JP reassured her as they hacked together back towards the stables. "But if you want to compete or play in any of the school tournaments then you'll definitely need them."

"Do you ride Luhmuhlen ponies?" Georgie asked.

"Me?" JP looked a bit insulted. "No, I've got my own string. I keep them stabled with the Luhmuhlen ponies though."

"So, if you've played in Argentina does that mean you're a really good player?" Georgie asked.

"My family all play polo so I've been on the circuit during the school holidays," JP said. "Players get graded between minus-two and ten. Ten goals is the best – there's hardly any ten-goal players in the world. My dad is a six-goal player and I'm a two-goal player – which is pretty good for someone who's just about to turn fourteen..."

There was a thunder of hooves across the fields. Georgie looked up and saw James Kirkwood riding towards them at a flat gallop on his polo mare. When he reached Georgie and JP he pulled the mare up to an abrupt stop alongside them.

"Hey, Georgie," James said, trying to act casual as if he hadn't just done a mad gallop to catch her. "I didn't know you were a polo player."

"I just started playing," Georgie said. "It's my new option subject."

"Georgie's just joined my class," JP added.

James narrowed his eyes suspiciously at JP. "How are things, John-Patrick?"

"Same as," JP responded.

"I hope you weren't boring Georgie with your stories about what a polo hero you are?" James said. Then, with his voice dripping sarcasm he added, "Like you're the big two-goal superstar!"

JP frowned. "What's your problem, Kirkwood? I was just showing Georgie a few moves."

"I bet you were." James looked indignant. "Well she doesn't need your help. In case you hadn't heard I'm due to get regraded mid-season so I'll be two goals as well. I think I'm qualified to take over Georgie's training schedule from here."

"Geez, dude," JP raised his hands in mock surrender. "We were just playing a bit of stick-and-ball. There's no need to go all alpha male on me."

JP turned to Georgie. "Listen, I better go. I'll see you in class, OK?"

"Really?" Georgie said, "I'm sorry about this…"

"Hey, no, it's cool," JP backed his horse away. "I have to feed my ponies anyway. I'll catch you later, OK?" He looked over at James who seemed to be smugly satisfied that JP was leaving. "See you around, Kirkwood."

"Not if I see you first," James shot back.

As soon as JP was out of earshot, Georgie rounded on James.

"What was all that about? What have you got against JP?"

"He was flirting with you," James said huffily.

"We were having stick-and-ball." Georgie was exasperated. "Alex and Cam were playing with us too!"

She groaned. "I doubt JP will want to play with me again after that wig-out."

"I did you a favour," James said sulkily. "That guy is a total numnah."

"Well, don't do me any more favours," Georgie said. She turned her back on him and rode off towards the stables.

✳

Georgie was still fuming when she returned from the stables that evening to Badminton House. Who did James Kirkwood think he was? There was nothing going on between her and JP – and what did it have to do with James anyway? He was the one who had broken up with her and now he was acting as if he owned her.

Alice was lying on her bed as Georgie stormed into their room.

"You will not believe what James has just done!" Georgie fumed.

"Neither will you," Alice replied pointing to the envelope on Georgie's bed. "That arrived for you half an hour ago."

Inside the envelope were two tickets to the movies – *National Velvet* at the Lido cinema in Lexington. Along with the tickets there was a handwritten note from James.

Georgie,

This movie is a total classic – you're going to love it. I'll pick you up Sunday night at six. See you then – James.

Chapter Six

"So it's all back on again with you and James?" Alice asked as she watched Georgie examine the movie tickets.

"No!" Georgie was still in shock. "I mean, maybe. Yes. Oh… I don't know!"

She threw herself down on her bed. "We had this fight on the polo fields. He got totally jealous seeing me hanging out with JP – which is crazy because there is zero going on between us. And now he sends me these tickets as if we'd already agreed to go to the movies together!"

"What about Riley?" Alice asked, casting a glance at the white flowers that were now wilting in their vase on Georgie's bedside cabinet.

Georgie sighed. "He turns up with a bunch of flowers, and he says he'll call me and then nothing!"

"Erm, you were the one who sent him away, remember?" Alice pointed out. "If you want to see him again, then you should call him."

"Really?" Georgie said. "Do you think so?"

The truth was, she had picked up the phone half a dozen times now to make the call and then lost her nerve. She didn't want to look like a stalker and the last thing he had said was that he would call her. So why hadn't he?

There was a knock on the bedroom door and Emily and Daisy both came in.

Emily saw the distraught look on Georgie's face. "What's wrong?"

"Georgie's having boy trouble," Alice announced.

"Who with?" Emily asked. "James or Riley?"

"Both," Georgie groaned.

Daisy looked deeply uninterested until Alice added, "James saw her playing polo with JP and made a total scene."

"You're playing polo?" Daisy suddenly perked up.

"Uh-huh," Georgie said. "It's my new option subject."

"How come you get to play? Why wasn't I asked to join?"

Daisy's competitive streak was barely concealed at the best of times, and at the mention of this new pursuit it was obvious that her nose was put out of joint that she wasn't involved. On the driveway on the way to dinner that evening she grilled Georgie about the basics of polo and how she had managed to wangle her way into Heath Brompton's class. By the time the girls reached the quad, Daisy was adamant that she wanted to give it a go too.

In the dinner queue she raced straight up to Cameron and Alex, dragging Emily along with her.

"What is she up to?" Alice asked Georgie as they took their trays to the table and sat down. A few moments later they were joined by Daisy, Emily and the boys.

"Guess what? We're playing polo!" Emily blurted out.

"What?" Alice said. "All of us?"

"We're going to play you," Cameron confirmed. "JP and Mark can play with us so we'll have four on each side. And you can borrow the Luhmuhlen polo gear."

Daisy looked thrilled. "It's all sorted. We're going to meet up on the fields tomorrow after school."

"We'll have a chuck together before dinner!" Emily said.

Alex shook his head. "It's a *chukk-a*," he corrected her with a grin. "You say 'we're having chukkas before dinner'."

"Oh, whatever!" Emily was bright-eyed. "I don't care if we're chucking up our dinner! It's going to be awesome!"

✴

Polo was all the girls could talk about at school the next day. Daisy was utterly obsessed and had spent the night before swotting up on all the polo websites. She was in ultra-competitive mode, and when they finally met up with the boys at the stables she insisted that Village Voice was too big and heavy to use and had begged Alex and Cameron to lend her one of Luhmuhlen House's polo ponies.

Georgie suspected that this was because Daisy hated to lose and knew she stood a better chance on a proper schooled polo pony.

Emily, on the other hand, was happy to ride her black

Thoroughbred Barclay. She was tacking him up in polo gear, which she had borrowed from Alex who was by her side helping her to fit it. Since the School Formal Emily and Alex were officially boyfriend and girlfriend, although the pair of them were so painfully shy that this mostly involved nothing more than sitting together at lunchtimes – which was what they used to do anyway.

Emily stood by and watched as Alex adjusted the standing martingale for her and did up the surcingle on the polo saddle.

"Do you want some help tacking up?" Cameron asked Alice.

"Are you kidding me?" Alice seemed to know exactly what she was doing as she expertly attached the martingale and strapped on tendon boots front and back.

She tightened her girth and stuck her foot into the stirrup, swinging up into the saddle.

"Do you want me to show you how to hold the reins?" Cameron asked.

"It's OK," Alice said, taking a grip on the two sets of reins and entwining them precisely between the fingers of her left hand in a perfect English Bridge. "I think I've got it."

She reached down and plucked a mallet out of the barrel in the corner of the stables, winding the lash expertly round her thumb and holding the stick perfectly as if she had been born with one in her hand.

"You've done this before then?" Cameron said.

"Yeah, we've got some ponies at home," Alice replied.

Alice had mentioned this to Georgie before, but it was only today that everyone realised the true extent of her abilities.

As soon as she was on the field Alice began manoeuvring Will with one hand like a professional, weaving up and down the field in an effortless rising canter as she struck the ball back and forth.

Georgie was stunned. "Why didn't you tell us that you could play?"

"I did!" Alice said. "I told you that me and my sisters used to play with Dad all the time back in Maryland."

"I thought you meant, like, just fooling around, not like a real game," Georgie admitted.

Alice looked at her as if she was mad. "Come on,

Georgie. You've met my family. Can you imagine Dad taking it easy on us kids? Our games at home are, like, crazy-competitive. Dad was on the national team before he married Mom and settled down on the farm. He's a total maniac with a mallet!"

It ran in the family. With a polo stick in her hands, Alice was like a trained ninja assassin. She cantered up and down the sidelines working on her swing.

Daisy eyed her technique jealously and then began to work in her own pony, a little fifteen-hand bay mare called Lucy.

Lucy was a 'made' pony –which meant that she was well trained and knew precisely what to do on the polo field. Lucy fell into a polo canter and maintained a steady lope, even on a loose rein as Daisy got comfortable practising her stops and turns.

Daisy looked quite smug with her progress until Georgie handed her the polo stick.

Daisy reached out her left hand to take it, but Georgie shook her head. "You have to use your right hand."

"But I'm left-handed," Daisy said.

"Not on the polo field," Georgie told her. "It's illegal

to play left-handed. You'll have to swap to your right hand like everyone else."

JP showed Daisy how to hold the reins and stick and she quickly adapted to her new right-handed grip. Meanwhile Alex was showing Emily how to take a forehand shot – she seemed quite tentative, but when she finally laid the mallet to the ball it went for miles.

"Wow!" Alex was impressed. "You've got a great swing!"

"Are we ready to play a chukka now?" JP asked.

"How are we splitting up the teams?" Cameron asked.

"Girls against boys," Alice said.

"We're ready. Let's do it!" Daisy raised her mallet in the air like a sword in challenge.

As the two teams took to the field Georgie, who had been devouring *How to Play Polo* since she borrowed it from the school library the week before, took charge of the girls' team strategy.

"Daisy, you're upfront in number one position," she instructed. "Your job is to attack the goal."

Daisy looked extremely pleased about this. Georgie didn't burst her bubble by telling her that the number one position was traditionally allocated to the Patron – the player who paid for the team's expenses but wasn't actually a great player.

The player in the number three jersey is the star rider on the team and the one in the most pivotal role. The number three is a goal shooter, but they are also responsible for covering the field and fighting for possession.

"Alice," Georgie instructed, "you should go in at three."

Emily was deployed to the back of the field at number four.

"It's a defensive position," Georgie explained. "Your job is to protect the goal." Georgie was at number two, a roaming position. It was her responsibility to keep the ball moving forward, passing to Alice and Daisy upfront.

When the girls had been practising stick-and-ball the atmosphere on the field had been light-hearted and silly as they giggled at mistimed strokes and flubbed hits. But now, as they arranged themselves in the lineout, they all had their game faces on.

There was no ref to throw the ball in to start them off so JP tossed it down the lineout. Alex was first to get his stick to it and he struck it cleanly down the field. Emily was immediately off after it on Barclay, running down the ball. She swung at it, but misjudged her shot and missed entirely. There were screams from the other girls on the team as Cameron and Alex both closed in and threatened to snatch the ball for a quick early goal. Emily didn't lose her cool though. She quickly regained her line on the ball and took a second swing, keeping her shoulder loose like Alex had shown her, and this time she struck the ball cleanly and sent it flying back up the pitch towards the halfway mark.

Everyone turned their ponies to give chase and there was a thundering of hooves as they galloped hard down on the ball.

Georgie suddenly found herself in the thick of the pack, ponies on either side of her as she urged Belle on into a gallop, the mare stretching out with every stride. It was like being in a horse race, except much more crowded – plus you knew that you were going to have to come to a screeching halt at any moment and take a swipe at the small white ball that was whizzing ahead of you up the field!

Determined to be the first one to the ball, Daisy was urging her polo pony into the lead, and just as Cameron was about to take a strike at it, Daisy cut in front of him and swung wildly with her mallet.

"Foul!" Cameron raised his stick in the air, and Alex and JP and Mark raised their sticks in unison.

"What are you talking about?" Daisy said indignantly pulling her horse up.

"You fouled me!" Cameron said. "That was dangerous play, you can't swing across in front of me like that!"

"OK, OK," Daisy said, "I get it."

Her dangerous play had cost them. The Luhmuhlen boys were given a penalty shot and Cameron took it, nudging the ball from the thirty-yard line, shooting deftly between the goal posts.

A few moments later Emily and Daisy were totally confused when the boys raced off with the ball and shot for the goal at the opposite end.

"But that's our goal!" Emily complained.

"No, it's not," Alice explained. "You swap ends after every goal."

It was only four minutes into the chukka, but already the ponies were sweating and heaving from their mad gallops back and forth up the field.

As the girls headed back to the lineout the score was two-nil against them.

"We need to get a goal," Georgie said.

"Well, duhh!" Daisy shot back.

Georgie ignored this. "Daisy, you need to stay with JP. Don't worry about where the ball is, just mark JP. He's their best player – we need to take him out of the game."

"OK," Daisy said to Georgie.

"Alice," Georgie turned to her, "you're the best player of any of us so stop holding back. Get in there and attack."

"What about me?" Emily asked.

"You keep back and protect the goal," Georgie told her. "If the ball comes near you then hit it as hard as you can back up the field. Aim for Alice. She knows what to do."

With their tactics sorted, the girls went into the lineout once more. This time, when the ball was thrown in by Cameron it was Alice who got to it first, passing it out to her team mates.

"Mine!" Georgie yelled, charging the ball and striking it quickly a second and then a third time.

She passed the ball to Daisy, but it flew straight past her and over the back line. No goal.

The boys were in possession once again. Alex knocked it in, with a hard shot that drove the ball sixty yards up the field to Mark, who made a pass to Cameron. Cameron was lining up the ball when Alice swooped down out of nowhere and knee-barged him off his line to steal the shot, driving it with a backhand to Daisy. This time, Daisy managed to get her reins and stick sorted and tapped the ball forward, then chased after it, fending off JP and striking the ball once more towards the goal. The line was smooth and straight and the ball went right between the posts.

"Goal!"

The girls' team went wild. It was two to one – they were back in the game!

Back on the centre line, the boys had possession again and Cameron was just about to take a shot at the goal posts when Alice appeared, barging him again and stealing the ball off him for a second time.

"Will you stop doing that?" Cameron scowled at her and rode his mare hard after her, determined to get the ball back. "It isn't funny!"

He caught up with Alice and rode for the ball, leaning right out of the saddle to swing his mallet. It would have been a good shot if Alice hadn't been too quick for him and flicked it with the lightning-fast swipe that sent it further down the field towards the goal mouth.

The whole pack turned to chase the ball down. This time the sound of hooves was almost drowned out by the shouts of the players themselves.

"Get out of the way!" Cam yelled at Alice.

Alice responded by knee-barging him once again, neck-reining Will hard to the side and clashing shoulder-to-shoulder with Cameron's pony, who fell away and let Alice take possession.

"That was a foul!" Cam raised his stick in the air.

"No, it wasn't!" Alice shouted back. She kept riding

and passed the ball to Georgie, who stopped the ball and then took a shot at the posts. The shot dribbled forward pathetically and rolled to a stop right in front of the posts.

"Hit it again!" Alice yelled out.

Georgie rode Belle forward and swung again and this time the ball flew through the air, square between the posts.

The game was over – the girls had the final goal!

✳

"That was the most fun I have had in, like, forever!" Alice said as the girls rode back to the stables.

"You were pretty harsh on Cameron," Georgie said. "That last goal when you rode him off the ball was hardcore."

"But you told me to do it, Georgie!" Alice frowned. "The other day when we were talking about me and Cam, you said I should try and do something to make him notice me!"

Georgie groaned. "Alice, I don't think beating him at polo was quite what I had in mind!"

Daisy agreed. "As a general rule, boys don't want to go out with girls who are always beating them at stuff."

"It's not my fault that I'm a better polo player than he is," Alice grumbled.

"It's a good idea to let boys win occasionally," Daisy said airily. "It keeps them happy."

"Anyway – it was brilliant fun and we should do it again," Emily said. "I was only just getting the hang of it when the chukka was over."

"We need four ponies each so we can have a proper game," Alice said.

"I don't see why the girls' houses don't have their own polo strings," Daisy harrumphed. "My parents pay the same school fees as the boys do – so how come they get one and we don't?"

Emily shrugged. "It's just tradition."

"You know what," Georgie said, "I'm a little bit tired of that excuse. Everything stupid here is 'tradition'. I don't see why there can't be a girls' team."

"They'd never provide us with sixteen ponies," Emily pointed out. "It would be far too expensive."

Alice agreed. "My dad has polo ponies and they cost a bomb. His good ones are worth about twenty thousand dollars apiece."

"But what if they just allocated the stabling?" Georgie argued. "If we had the same facilities as the boys and we were responsible for getting our own string of ponies together?"

Alice perked up. "I could ask my dad for some ponies! He'd never let me have his best competition mares, but he's got, like, half a dozen old polo mares that he's retired."

"And we could use our own horses," Georgie added. "That's another four."

"I'm not using Village Voice," Daisy said. "I mean, I'm not trying to be a handbrake or anything but he's just too big to ride polo on."

"Well we've got three horses then, plus the ponies that Alice says we could get from her dad..." Georgie did the maths.

"We've got a few polo ponies at home too," Emily offered, "but I don't think my dad could afford to ship them over from New Zealand."

"So they have polo ponies in New Zealand?" Alice asked.

"Loads!" Emily said. "They use Thoroughbreds – any mares that don't grow big enough to be raced on the track often end up being sold on as polo ponies."

"They use actual racehorses?" Daisy said.

"Well, smaller ones," Emily said. "I know a place back home where they retrain racehorses that used to gallop."

"Ohmygod!" Georgie's eyes went wide. "I've got a totally genius idea! I know where we can get enough Thoroughbreds to start our own string!"

At that moment the sound of hooves echoed through the stables up ahead of them and, round the corner, three riders appeared. At the front of the group, riding a sleek golden chestnut, was a girl with glossy red hair.

"Kennedy alert! Let's get out of here," Alice muttered.

"Where to?" Georgie hissed back. "She's already seen us. Keep calm, she's like a shark – she can smell fear."

"I thought sharks smelled blood and horses smelled fear?" Emily murmured.

"Sharks can smell dogs if they're in the water," Daisy offered.

Georgie groaned. "Not the point, guys."

Now it was really too late to escape. Better to face the enemy head-on.

"Hello, Kennedy," Georgie said.

The only good thing about being kicked out of eventing class was that Georgie had hardly seen Kennedy Kirkwood so far this term. OK, the showjumperettes were still in the same class as Georgie for maths and German – but Georgie made sure that she arrived late and sat across the other side of the room. She had caught glimpses of Kennedy at lunchtimes, looking ridiculously perfect, like she had a team of hairdressers summoned to her dorm room each morning. The head showjumperette was a Ralph Lauren ad come to life. Even the drab regulation winter uniform looked good the way she wore it, with her kilt skirt shortened into a mini.

The other showjumperettes wore their uniform the same way as Kennedy. She was their leader and they idolised her from the top of their blow-dried heads to the tips of their fingers – which had been painted in Kennedy's new favourite shade – Chanel 'grey 505 particuliere'.

But right now there was only one thing about Kennedy's style statement that Georgie noticed – her jacket. Kennedy was wearing Georgie's Barbour.

"Ohmygod. That's my coat!" Georgie never thought the showjumperette would actually have the nerve to wear it at school!

"You mean it *was* your coat," Kennedy smirked. "My boyfriend gave it to me."

"Give it back right now, Kennedy," Georgie said.

"Or you'll what?" Kennedy said. "What exactly can you do, Georgie? My boyfriend is the head prefect of Burghley House."

"Wow," Alice said, "I never thought I'd actually meet someone who was proud to admit they dated Conrad."

Kennedy's face turned dark with anger and she was about to snap back at Alice when Arden suddenly interrupted. "Hey! Why are you guys dressed like that?"

"Like what?" Alice asked.

"Like polo players," Arden said.

"Because, Arden," Alice said, as if she were talking to a five-year-old, "we have been playing polo."

"You're kidding!" Arden giggled.

"It's not a joke," Georgie said. "We've formed a girls' team."

Arden was still giggling. "You look stupid. Polo is a boys' game."

Georgie glared at her. "Arden, you can stand on the sidelines like a stick chick if you want, but some of us are actually interested in playing."

"It's not a proper team though, is it?" Tori said, taking Arden's side. "You're not real polo players."

"Yes, we are." Georgie suddenly lost her cool. "In fact, Badminton House is getting its own polo string."

The other three girls looked wide-eyed at her.

"You're lying," Kennedy said.

"No, I'm not." Georgie was shaking. "I've been talking to the headmistress about starting a new girls' team. She's pretty keen on the idea."

"No way!" Kennedy still didn't believe her. "This is Blainford Academy. Hell will freeze over before they give permission for a girls' polo team."

"Well, get your pitchfork ready for a snowball fight, Kennedy, because we are totally forming a Blainford girls' polo team – we're going to be playing in the Round Robin Tournament at the end of the month!" Alice retorted.

"Oh, what-ever!" Kennedy rolled her eyes and looked over at Arden and Tori. "Let's get out of here."

As the showjumperettes rode away Alice let out a groan. "And there it is, everyone! The sound of my pathetic hollow threat echoing through the stables."

Georgie shook her head. "That wasn't a threat, it was a promise. We have to start a team now – even if it's just to get back at Kennedy!"

"Totally," Daisy agreed.

"Uh, I hate to be a downer," Emily said, "but don't we have to, like, get permission first?"

"You heard what Georgie said," Daisy replied. "She's already been to talk to the headmistress about it!"

"Yes, but that was a lie, wasn't it?" Emily said.

"Um, yeah," Georgie admitted. "But it's about to become true."

She looked at the other girls.

"I'm going to see Mrs Dickins-Thomson first thing in the morning."

Chapter Seven

Mrs Dickins-Thomson's office was on the upper level of the main building, directly above the library. The ancient wood-panelled room smelled of violets and horse leather. Harnesses, antique stock whips and various pieces of unusual equine paraphernalia were hung on the walls.

Directly over the vast walnut desk where Mrs Dickins-Thomson sat was an oil painting of a horse. He wasn't exactly a ravishing beauty. Even the untrained eye could see that the horse was a rather donkey-ish sort. He was plain brown in colour, with no white markings to speak of and a heavy head, a bit like a Wellington boot with big ears.

This oil painting was well-known by most of the

senior pupils at Blainford. It was a bit of a rite of passage for Mrs Dickins-Thomson to sit her pupils down in the chair facing her desk and ask them to tell her the name of the horse in the painting. And this morning Georgie was in the hotseat.

"Can you tell me who the horse is, Miss Parker?" Mrs Dickins-Thomson asked.

Georgie shifted uncomfortably. She had never laid eyes on the painting before now and the horse seemed entirely unremarkable.

"I'm afraid I don't know, Miss Dickins-Thomson," Georgie said.

"I'll give you a clue," the headmistress said. "He's a famous racehorse, who won the match race of the century, beating the great stallion War Admiral to the post in nineteen-thirty-eight."

"Really?" Georgie said.

"You seem surprised, Miss Parker."

"Well, he doesn't look up to much, does he?"

Mrs Dickins-Thomson smiled. "No, he doesn't," she agreed. "If horseracing was based on looks, his chances would have been slim." The headmistress walked over to the painting and Georgie noticed that the brown tweed of her coat matched the colours in the portrait. Mrs Dickins-Thomson looked a little bit like a horse herself, with her long face and aquiline nose.

"His name was Seabiscuit," Mrs Dickins-Thomson continued. "He was born undersized, a Thoroughbred foal with the worst conformation they'd ever seen at Claiborne Farm stud in Kentucky. He had knobby-knees and weak hocks. When they put him on the track he failed to win his first ten races – most of the time running dead last."

"I thought you said he was a famous racehorse?" Georgie frowned.

"Oh, that came much later," Mrs Dickins-Thomson said. "You see, Seabiscuit might not have looked like a star in the beginning, but underneath his humble exterior he had huge heart.

"Everything changed when he was sold to a new owner and suddenly he became a racing legend. Seabiscuit beat the mighty War Admiral head-to-head in a match race, outrunning him by four lengths. He won all the big races including the Santa Anita Handicap –

in fact, there is a life-sized bronze statue of him at the Santa Anita track."

Mrs Dickins-Thomson put a hand up to the painting and traced her finger along the horse's muzzle. "Seabiscuit needed the people around him to nurture the greatness that was hidden within. It wasn't until others believed in him and worked hard to bring out the best that he could truly shine. That is our task here at Blainford Academy. We must believe in our riders, train and guide them so that they too can become stars."

Mrs Dickins-Thomson stared at the painting for a moment longer and then she shook herself out of her reverie.

"Anyway, Miss Parker, what can I do for you today?"

"I want to start a girls' polo team," Georgie said.

✸

It was pitch-black at 5am when the pick-up truck pulled up outside the Badminton House dormitory. Nervous that Riley would honk and wake the whole place up, Georgie ran down the stairs to meet him.

Riley leapt out of the truck and came around to open the passenger door and it was then that he realised she wasn't alone. Alice, Daisy and Emily were trooping down the stairs behind her.

"They're coming too?" Riley looked surprised.

"I'm sorry," Georgie said. "I thought I'd mentioned it. I hope you don't mind?"

"Of course not," Riley said, "I just don't know how I'm supposed to fit all of you in the pick-up."

"Don't worry about it," Emily joined them on the driveway, "I can ride on the back. I do it on the farm at home."

"Me too," Alice said, grabbing the side of the truck and hoisting herself up on to the flatbed alongside Emily while Daisy took the other seat inside the cab next to Georgie.

"Are you sure?" Riley said to Emily and Alice. "It's freezing. You'll be icicles by the time we get there."

"It's not that far," Emily said. "We'll be fine."

"Hold on a second." Riley reached over to a stack of Hessian sacks. "There's an old horse rug under this stuff. Throw that over yourselves to keep warm."

The girls snuggled together on the flatbed, hunkering down beneath the rug.

"Just knock on the window if it gets too cold, OK?" Riley said, as he opened the driver's door.

He jumped into the cab beside Georgie. "So what's this all about?" He turned to her. "Why are you girls suddenly so desperate to go and watch trackwork at Keeneland Park?"

Georgie dug into the pocket of her coat and pulled out an envelope. She opened it up and showed Riley. It was full of hundred-dollar bills. "We're buying horses."

✳

Georgie had laid out her plan to the other Badminton House girls after they ran into Kennedy Kirkwood wearing the stolen Barbour.

"All the trainers take their Thoroughbreds to Keeneland Park for trackwork on a Saturday morning. We'll turn up and watch the horses train and figure out which mares are too small and too slow to race. Then we'll buy them off the trainers and school them up into polo ponies."

"It's a genius plan," Daisy agreed. "Except for the bit where we buy the horses. I don't know about you guys, but I don't get enough pocket money to stretch to a string of polo ponies."

"Me neither," Emily said. "You heard what Alice said. A good polo mare can cost as much as twenty thousand dollars!"

"But we're not going to be buying the good ones," Georgie pointed out. "We're looking for the washed-up, useless racehorses that no one wants. We should be able to pick them up dirt cheap!"

"OK," Alice frowned. "So how much have we got?"

"I've got three hundred dollars in my savings account," Emily offered.

"I've got the cash my nana gave me at Christmas and my savings – that's almost five hundred pounds," said Daisy. "What about you, Georgie?"

Georgie looked at her friends. "Are we really serious about this? We're going to start our own polo team?"

"Totally," Alice confirmed.

Georgie took a deep breath. "I can get the money," she said, "I just need to talk to my dad…"

Her phone call back home started out all right. Dr Parker had just walked in the door and was having his Friday night glass of brandy, which always put him in a good mood. But the tone of his voice changed abruptly when he discovered the reason for the call.

"Let me get this straight," her dad said. "You want to buy a squad of ponies?"

"Not a squad, Dad, a string," Georgie said. "Alice's dad is giving us six of his old mares, and we already have our own horses, so I only need another three ponies for me."

"Oh, so it's just three?" Dr Parker said sarcastically. "Right, where do I sign the cheque?"

"You don't have to sign a cheque, Dad," Georgie said. "I've got my own money from selling Tyro. I'm just asking you to let me spend it."

There was a pause on the other end of the line. "I'm getting three for the price of one, so it's saving money in a way," Georgie pointed out. "Plus we're going to school them up so they'll be worth more – it's like an investment."

In the end, Georgie's strange logic and her dogged persistence wore Dr Parker down.

"All right," he told her. "How much are the other girls' parents letting them spend?"

"Well, Daisy has five hundred pounds…"

"Fine. Then you can have the same," Dr Parker said. "That ought to be enough for three ponies."

"But—"

"Georgie, don't push your luck. Take the offer and hang up now," Dr Parker cautioned her.

"OK, thanks, Dad."

As Georgie hung up the phone she realised she was shaking. Her dad was wiring her five hundred pounds. She was going pony shopping!

✳

The guard at the gates of the Keeneland Park track knew Kenny's red pick-up truck by sight, although he was a little surprised when the truck pulled up and Riley was behind the wheel.

"Morning, Riley, where's your uncle Kenny?" the guard asked.

"Hey, Earl," Riley leaned out the window of the truck. "Still in bed, probably."

The guard shone his torchlight on to the flatbed where Emily and Alice were sitting under the horse rug and then shifted the beam into the cab of the pick-up where Georgie and Daisy were sitting alongside Riley.

"Does Kenny know that you're using his truck to transport a herd of fillies?" the guard said with a grin.

Riley looked embarrassed. "Can I drive on through, Earl?"

"Sure you can, son. Park up by the stables. I think your father is already here."

Riley eased the pick-up through the gates and steered it towards the ivy-covered limestone buildings up ahead to the left.

"Your dad is here?" Georgie asked.

"Yeah," Riley nodded. "We've got a couple of horses in work at the moment – I'm riding track for him today so I'll have to abandon you guys for a while."

"It's OK," Georgie smiled at him, "I know my way around."

She had been to Keeneland Park before to try her hand at riding trackwork for Riley's dad. Now that she was back here, smelling the familiar scents of the horse sweat, liniment and tobacco, and listening to the jockeys' voices floating out of the darkness, she wished she was about to mount up too.

Riley parked the truck and headed for the stables on foot, and Georgie led the girls over to the railings where the bright spotlights above the track illuminated the jockeys mounted up on their first rides of the day. On the sidelines by the white wooden railings the trainers stood in their heavy overcoats, binoculars dangling round their necks, with stopwatches clasped in their hands.

As they approached the railings one of the men in a brown wool coat and baggy corduroy breeches turned round to give Georgie a wave. "Georgie Parker!"

"Hi, Mr Conway."

"Riley told me you were coming out with him this morning," John Conway smiled at her. "I hoped you might be considering riding trackwork for me again? Clarise sure could do with a jockey."

Georgie smiled. "Thanks, but I'm not here to ride today, I'm here to buy some horses."

John Conway looked taken aback. "You're planning to become a racehorse owner?"

"Oh, no!" Georgie shook her head. "We're looking for Thoroughbreds that are too small and too slow for the track."

Georgie introduced Alice, Daisy and Emily to Mr Conway. "The four of us are starting a girls' polo team and we need horses," she explained.

"So what are you looking for?" John Conway asked.

"Fifteen-two hands and under," Daisy ran through their checklist on her fingers, "any colour, with strong muscly hindquarters, short-coupled and short pasterned, but long-necked—"

"And they've got to be cheap," Georgie added.

The girls leaned up against the railings with Mr Conway and watched the horses being breezed.

"That brown mare looks good," Alice said, pointing to a horse that was being taken down to the sixth furlong marker by her jockey.

"She is good," John Conway said. "Too good for you. That's one of my mares – Scandal. I'm expecting her to run in the Oaks this summer."

He pointed over at a skinny-legged chestnut that was currently putting up a fight on the concourse as his jockey tried to convince him to step out on to the sandy loam of the track.

"Now that's more your speed. That chestnut is one of Tommy Doyle's horses. He's run in three graded races so far since he turned three years old – and he's been last in every single one of them."

"No surprise," Daisy said. "He looks like he doesn't even want to set foot on the track!"

The little chestnut Thoroughbred was putting up such a fuss, it took two handlers, one on either side holding his bridle, to convince him to leave the concourse.

Once he was out on the track the little chestnut showed no more inclination to move forward than he did before. When his jockey attempted to ride him round the track at a steady gallop, the horse kept napping and at one point he actually stopped dead in his tracks and spun round!

"Did you see that?" Alice was wide-eyed.

"Well at least we know he can turn," Daisy said.

"Yeah, but do we want a gelding?" Emily asked. "I thought they had to be mares."

Georgie watched as the chestnut pulled up to a halt

and a man in a grey tweed coat walked over with a stern look on his face to talk to the jockey.

"I say if the price is right, then a gelding is fine," Georgie said.

She turned to Mr Conway. "Is that Tommy Doyle?"

John Conway nodded. "Right now, I'd say if you were to offer him the price of a bullet it would save him the cost of putting one in that horse."

"Is he kidding?" Emily whispered, horrified.

Georgie knew that John Conway's comment probably wasn't far off the truth. A gelding that didn't have any value as a racehorse couldn't even be turned out to breed more colts and fillies. If he couldn't run then he was useless and worthless.

"I'll be back in a second," Georgie told the others. She ducked under the railings of the fence and strode out across the track towards Tommy Doyle and the skinny chestnut Thoroughbred.

Tommy Doyle was a short, stocky man. From his height Georgie guessed that he had probably been a jockey once, but you could tell by his width that it must have been a long time ago. He wore his fedora cap low over his sunken eyes, and he pushed the hat back now so he could get a good look at the young girl who was walking towards him, calling his name.

"Mr Doyle?" Georgie smiled. "Hi, I'm Georgie Parker. I'm a friend of John Conway's."

Tommy Doyle nodded. "Listen, miss, whatever girl-guide club you're selling cookies for, can this wait? I've got my hands full at the moment here."

Georgie wasn't about to be put off. "Mr Conway told me your horse has come last in all three of his races so far."

"He told you that, did he?" Tommy Doyle didn't exactly look thrilled to hear it. Georgie realised she'd better cut to the chase before he told her to get lost.

"I'm looking to buy polo ponies and I thought that since he wasn't doing so well as a racehorse you might want to sell him to me."

Tommy Doyle looked at her in disbelief. "Are you trying to make me an offer on my horse?"

"Uh-huh," Georgie said. "If you're interested in selling him."

"Oh, he's for sale all right." Tommy Doyle took his

hat off and ran a hand through his oiled-back hair. "What sort of money are we talking about?"

Georgie took a deep breath. "A hundred and fifty dollars."

It was a cheeky offer and she knew it, but as far as she was concerned she had nothing to lose. Right now the chestnut gelding standing in front of her was on a major losing streak.

Tommy Doyle put his hat back on and looked Georgie in the eyes. "I'll sell him to you for five hundred," he said.

"Two hundred is my best offer," Georgie replied.

"Four hundred."

Georgie took the envelope out of her coat pocket. "Two hundred – cash in your hand and I'll take the horse with me."

Tommy Doyle shook his head in disbelief. *The bare-faced cheek of this girl!*

He put out his hand for Georgie to shake. "You've got a deal," he said.

✷

Georgie was shaking with excitement as she walked back over to the other girls. "I just bought a horse!"

The others couldn't believe it when Georgie told them the bargain price she had paid.

"What's his name?" Emily asked.

"I don't know," Georgie had to admit. "I forgot to ask!"

The chestnut's name turned out to be Saratoga Firefly.

"Well, that's his racing name," the jockey told the girls as he unsaddled the little chestnut and handed Daisy the reins, "but back at the yard we call him Spinner."

"Why?"

"He likes to turn round in mid-gallop. Does a full one-eighty on the track!"

"He's got good conformation," Daisy assessed. "Look at those hindquarters."

"He's got a keen look in his eyes too," Emily agreed. "Haven't you, Spinner?"

"I don't think we should call him that," Georgie said, stroking the chestnut's face. "He needs a proper polo pony name. Something short and easy to remember on the field."

"How about Lucky?" Alice suggested, "As in, he's lucky he's not pet food."

"How about Marco?" Emily suggested. "You know, like Marco Polo?"

The others groaned at the joke, but the name seemed to stick.

"How are we going to get him home?" Alice asked. "He's too big to fit on the back of the pick-up with me and Emily."

"Mr Conway has offered to truck the ponies for us," Georgie said. "He says he can fit seven ponies onboard."

Daisy dug her cash out of her pocket. "I better start shopping," she said to the others. "I'll meet you back here later with my new polo string."

Emily followed along after Daisy. Georgie and Alice took Marco off to tie him up to the Conways' truck, and by the time they returned to the railside there was a new group of Thoroughbreds coming out for their trackwork.

In amongst the group of jockeys Riley emerged on to the track on a big black horse that Georgie recognised straight away.

"That's Talisman." She pointed the big, black gelding out to Alice. "I rode him the last time I was here."

Georgie gave Riley a wave as he rode past and he diverted course and brought Talisman over to the railings.

"Have you bought anything yet?" he asked.

"One chestnut gelding," Georgie said.

"I thought they had to be mares?"

"We've loosened up our criteria," Alice replied.

Riley nodded. "I've been asking around in the stables. Apparently Bart O'Malley has a couple of horses that have been on a mean losing streak."

"Which ones are they?" Georgie asked.

Riley scanned the track. "Look for Bart's stable colours – purple and red diamonds. I can't see them out here right now. But they'll be around."

He smiled at Georgie. "I better go breeze Tally before Dad catches me slacking off."

"Thanks for the tip," Georgie said. She watched Riley as he rode off at a trot on Talisman. When he reached the first furlong marker Riley rose up into his stirrups, asking Talisman to move up into a gallop, and then he began to work the horse round the track.

Riley was a naturally confident rider, utterly at ease in the saddle. He never seemed to do much, but somehow he got the best out of a horse. She watched as he asked Talisman to step up the pace as they came round to the final three furlongs. As they passed another horse, a big bay, she saw Riley bend down a little lower over Tally's neck, his hands urging the big black on. Tally surged forward and now he was thundering home in the straight, Riley perched up on his back, looking like there was nowhere else in the world he would rather be. Georgie remembered that night at the School Formal when Riley had turned up out of the blue, all dressed up in a suit, his dark hair slicked back off his face. He'd come, despite his feelings about the snobbish Blainford elite, making the effort just to be with her. Now, watching him ride, she felt guilty for putting him through that. Riley didn't belong at Blainford. Out there on the track now, riding for all he was worth, that was Riley as he was meant to be. Was that why he hadn't called her after the dance? He'd always tried to tell her that they were from different worlds.

"Georgie?" Alice grabbed her arm. "Come on! Are you going to stand there staring at Riley all day or are we going to the stables to find these horses?"

✳

Bart O'Malley did have two mares that he was apparently trying to get rid of. There was a skittish young bay, only about fifteen hands high with not much in the way of muscle and a slight ewe neck.

"She'll be all right once we feed her up," Alice insisted. "I like her."

The other mare was a dark brown standing at fifteen-three, which made her a little big for polo, but the girls decided she would do.

"How much do you want for them?" Georgie asked the russet-haired trainer.

"Neither of them are going to win a race," Bart O'Malley admitted, "but the brown mare has good bloodlines. I could put her in foal and get a good colt out of her, so I'm in no hurry to sell."

"He's bluffing," Alice muttered to Georgie. "He wants to sell them – you can tell!"

Georgie frowned. "All I've got left is three hundred dollars for both horses," she said to O'Malley. She dug her hands in her coat pocket and showed him the envelope. "Cash money."

O'Malley shook his head. "Not enough," he said flatly.

"Walk away now!" Alice hissed to Georgie.

"What?" Georgie was shocked when Alice grabbed her arm and almost dragged her off.

"Fine by us!" Alice called back to O'Malley as she stormed off down the corridor with Georgie in tow. "There are other horses, you know!"

The girls had barely gone halfway down the corridor when O'Malley called them back.

"All right, all right! You got yourself a deal."

Georgie handed him the money and the girls took a horse each.

Georgie couldn't believe what had just happened. She'd never bought a horse before in her life and today she had just bought three!

"I hope this polo thing works out," she told Alice,

"otherwise I've just lumbered myself with three washed-up racehorses!"

"You're not the only one," Alice said. "Look!"

Daisy and Emily were walking towards them, each of them leading two horses.

"We've bought them!" Emily was trembling with excitement.

Georgie shook her head in disbelief. "I think we've all gone mad."

It wasn't until she was loading her three new Thoroughbreds on the truck that it occurred to her: Badminton House now had its own polo team – and it would never have happened if Kennedy Kirkwood had kept her paws off Georgie's Barbour!

Chapter Eight

*O*n the road back to Blainford Georgie and the other girls were full of stories of their wheeling and dealing. It wasn't until they were unloading the truck that the reality of what they had done finally struck them.

As Georgie watched Riley leading the Thoroughbreds down the ramp she felt a wave of fear rising up inside her. These weren't pony-club ponies – they were bona fide racehorses. They stood there twitching and trembling with nerves, their eyes out on stalks as they surveyed their new environment, and all Georgie could think was that this might be the biggest mistake of her life.

She didn't know a thing about training Thoroughbreds and transforming them into polo ponies. Daisy and Emily, both with two new horses apiece, didn't have a clue either! Between them, the girls had seven skinny, young creatures straight off the track, all gangly legs and wild eyes.

"They don't look like polo ponies, do they?" Georgie said.

"No," Daisy agreed. "They don't."

"OK, so they need an extreme makeover," Alice said, "but that's why they were so cheap."

Georgie wasn't so convinced. How were they going to train these Thoroughbreds for polo when it was hard enough to handle them on the ground?

The worst of the bunch by far was Marco. The chestnut gelding had been a nightmare to get on the horse truck in the first place and he came racing down the ramp tense and flighty. Georgie had to grapple with him to hold him still as Emily and Alice took the mares off to the other end of the stable block, and as soon as they were out of sight the gelding started going bonkers. Panicky about being left alone, he began whinnying, his head held high as he danced from side to side. It was almost impossible for Georgie to hold him as he swung his hindquarters about, trotting anxiously on the spot as if he had hot coals beneath his hooves.

"Give him here," Riley stepped in and took the leadrope out of Georgie's hands. "He shouldn't be allowed to get away with bad manners." He squared up to the gelding and spoke gently but firmly to him, giving a sharp pull on his halter to get his attention. Marco flung a foreleg out, defiantly striking at Riley, but the boy remained unrattled. He began to walk the horse alongside him round the yard. Marco had his ears back at first and kept trying to pull away, but every time the horse tried to act up, Riley was one step ahead of him, anticipating the Thoroughbred's next move and correcting him calmly but firmly until the gelding was walking docile as a lamb towards his loose box.

"He's not a bad horse," Riley insisted to Georgie as he opened the door to the loose box and let Marco inside, slipping his halter off and then bolting the bottom half of the door shut. "He's got real good bloodlines, but the jockeys in Tommy Doyle's stable didn't understand him. They let him think he was the boss." Marco turned round in his stall and came back to Riley now, ears pricked forward as he stuck his head over the door. "See?" Riley smiled as he gave Marco a pat. "He just needs to learn some respect and know his place."

"That's funny," a voice behind them said. "I was just thinking the same thing about you."

Georgie turned round and saw James Kirkwood standing there, glaring at Riley.

"I would have thought it would be common courtesy to ask permission before you walk in here as if you own the place."

"Are you kidding me?" Riley replied. He looked at Georgie. "Who is this guy?"

James stepped forward and abruptly stuck out his hand – as if he was a businessman introducing himself in a meeting instead of a fourteen-year-old boy. "I'm James Kirkwood," he said. "I don't think we've been introduced."

Riley looked at the hand and then reluctantly shook it. "I'm Riley Conway."

"Riley, Riley…" James said the name as if he was trying to remember where he'd heard it before. "Hey, you must be the guy who took Georgie to the School Formal?"

"Yeah," Riley said. "That's right."

"Riley is helping me with the horses," Georgie said.

"And you're helping yourself to the Burghley stables?" James said.

"Badminton House doesn't have its own stable block," Georgie replied. "We've got permission to be here. The headmistress told us to put them—"

Riley interrupted her explanation. "I don't think James really cares about the horses being in his stables, Georgie. I think he doesn't like the fact that I'm here with you. Isn't that right?"

James gave Riley a smart-alec look. "Hey, no. I think it's great that Georgie has got someone like you to do her menial work for her."

James had a cocky look on his face as he reached out and put his arm round Georgie's shoulders. "As long as my girl is happy, that's fine by me."

Georgie stiffened at this sudden display of affection, but James ignored her discomfort and kept his arm firmly round her, staring intently all the while at Riley.

"I better go now, Georgie," James said, releasing his grip at last. "I'll see you tomorrow night for our date. Pick you up at six?"

Georgie watched in astonishment as James sauntered off. Then she turned back to Riley. He looked really angry.

"You're going out with him? You have a date?" he asked her, his voice strained with disbelief.

Georgie didn't know what to say. "He bought cinema tickets."

"So now you're going to the movies with that snotty little trust-fund creep?" Riley said, looking hurt and bewildered.

Georgie got defensive. "Well, what was I supposed to do? Wait forever for you to pick up the phone?"

She could feel herself making the whole thing worse, but didn't know how to stop. "You never even called me after the Formal!"

Riley scowled at her. "And you only call me when you want help with your horses," he said. "James is right. As long as I know my place like the rest of the staff around here, everything will be just fine."

"What?" Georgie couldn't believe it. "Riley! Don't be stupid."

"Why not?" Riley shot back. "I feel pretty stupid right

now. Running around after you, getting you and your friends into Keeneland Park and helping you to buy your horses and all the while you've got your hot date lined up for tomorrow night."

"That is so not what it's like!" Georgie insisted. "You vanished off the face of the earth after the dance and then you turn up with flowers and then disappear all over again."

"Because," Riley said, his voice trembling with anger, "I knew it would be like this, Georgie. You're at this fancy school surrounded by rich kids like him and I don't fit in. How am I supposed to compete with a guy like James?"

Riley dropped the halter and leadrope to the ground as he walked away.

"I'll see you around, Georgie."

"Riley, wait!" Georgie called after him. "Don't go. I'm sorry, it's all my fault."

Riley turned round. "No, Georgie. It's my fault. I should never have turned up at the dance or brought you stupid flowers." He looked embarrassed. "I've gotta go."

"Riley, please."

But Riley wasn't listening. He had walked out of the stables and the next thing Georgie knew, she could hear the sound of the horse truck starting up. By the time she reached the doorway he was already steering the truck out of the main gates and driving away.

✳

"Well, I'm totally Team Riley," Emily announced at breakfast the next morning. "Who does James think he is?"

"Uh-uh," Daisy disagreed as she scooped up a forkful of scrambled eggs from her plate. "It'd be a total pain in the neck trying to date a boy who doesn't go to school here. You'd hardly ever see him, whereas if you go out with James you can see him all the time, plus he's good-looking and a really good rider."

"Uh, guys?" Georgie stared at them in disbelief. "I don't actually have a choice in the matter. Riley isn't even speaking to me!"

"Well that settles it," Daisy said triumphantly. "Team James wins."

Georgie groaned and pushed her bacon and eggs aside, her appetite completely gone.

"Where is Alice anyway?" Emily asked.

Alice, as it turned out, was already at the Burghley House stables. The girls found her there, talking to a man with a clipboard in his hands. The man was wearing a dark green shirt with the words *Billington's Transport* written on the pocket in curly gold embroidery.

His truck, which was parked outside, was also dark green with the same words painted on the side.

"Sign here," he told Alice, passing over the clipboard.

The man headed round the back of the truck to lower the ramp.

"What's going on?" Georgie asked.

"Dad's polo ponies have arrived!" Alice said.

"But where's your dad?"

"He was going to drive them here from Maryland himself, but he was too busy," Alice shrugged. "He put them on a transporter instead."

Georgie and Alice watched as the truck driver lowered the ramp.

"Any idea what horses are inside?"

"Nope," Alice said. "Dad's got so many polo ponies, I've pretty much lost track. Most are used as broodmares once they retire from competition, but some are too old to have foals, or aren't suitable for breeding. They've been turned out in the paddocks so Dad said I could use them."

As they were talking, the man in the green shirt stepped up the ramp to bring out the first two mares.

"Ohh," Alice said. "It's a bit like waiting to see what your Christmas gifts are, isn't it?"

The first two horses down the ramp were both chestnuts, and even though their manes were long and scraggly and their coats were coarse, Georgie could see that they were compact and muscular, with perfect conformation for playing polo.

"That one's Jada," Alice said pointing to the chestnut with the narrow white stripe on her nose. "She's an excellent polo mare. The other mare with the white star and the stocking on her near hind, is Estrella. They're both quite old, but they used to be two of Dad's fave ponies. He's had two foals out of each of them."

"Where do you want them?" the man asked Alice

as he stood at the bottom of the ramp holding the horses.

"Let's just tie them all up by the stable block for now," Alice said.

Georgie took the two chestnuts from the driver and tied them up while the man went back up the ramp. He emerged a moment later with the next two horses, a dark bay and a smallish-looking dun mare with a black dorsal stripe. When Alice saw the dun mare, she shrieked with delight.

"Ohmygod! It's Desiray!" She walked over to the little dun, who was only about fifteen hands high. "I was hoping Dad would send her! I learned to ride polo on Desiray – she's a Quarter Horse/Thoroughbred cross. She used to be Dad's best mare in her heyday – she was on the US team that won the Admiral's Cup."

Alice gave Desiray a firm pat on her rump and the mare put her ears flat back and stamped a hoof in anger at having her personal space violated. Alice giggled at her moody antics. "She's a bit grumpy on the ground, but she's still got all the moves – totally a made pony," Alice said.

The last two horses off the truck were both dark bays. "Vita and Violet," Alice said. Vita turned out to be the prettiest of the two, a mare with a perfect star on her forehead and with four white socks. "She's a really good galloper," Alice said, patting Vita on her neck.

"What about Violet?" Georgie asked.

"Violet, not so much," Alice rolled her eyes. "She's a bit of a slug actually. She wouldn't have been my first choice on the truck, let's put it that way."

They put the new mares away in their loose boxes next to the racehorses that they had bought at Keeneland the day before.

With the addition of Alice's six mares, the Badminton House ponies now occupied a large chunk of the Burghley House stalls. Georgie walked up and down the row, checking on the new horses. "It's so weird. We have an instant polo team."

Alice nodded. "If we count Dad's horses, the Thoroughbreds and Will, Belle and Barclay we've got enough to ride four horses each for four chukkas. We can put our name down on the Round Robin Tournament roster."

The Blainford Round Robin was the yearly school polo competition. It was held in two phases. The first round in three weeks' time was a knock-out competition, followed the next weekend by the finals.

"We'll never be ready that soon," Georgie pointed out. But Alice wasn't going to be dissuaded. Back at the boarding house she spent the rest of the morning composing a training schedule.

"We have to crack into training straight away if we're going to stand any chance," she told the others as they gathered round, trying to decipher the colour-coded grid that listed dates and riders' horses' names in various squares.

"I've made a timetable for each of us." Alice passed the bits of paper round the group. "We'll do stick-and-ball training every day after school. We're each working three horses every session, and I've rotated the horses between us so we should have them ready to play by the time the tournament begins."

"This is brilliant!" Emily was poring over her timetable, trying to understand it. "So, when does training actually begin?"

Alice pointed to the first square at the top of the page. "Today."

✳

The Dupree horses needed a day to recover from their long truck journey so the girls decided to trial their new Thoroughbred acquisitions first.

Georgie was relieved to see that the Thoroughbreds were more relaxed, having had a couple of days to settle into their new home. Their eyes were no longer out on stalks as they walked the Burghley House corridor, but they were still tense and twitchy as the girls tacked them up in their new gear – a complicated arrangement of gag bits, martingales and surcingles.

Emily wasn't certain about the new kit either.

"These saddles are weird," she said as she threw one across her mare's back. "They've got no kneepads."

"Polo saddles don't have kneepads," Alice said. "It makes it easier for the rider to move around to swing the stick."

Georgie's first mount for the day was the young bay

mare with the ewe neck that she had bought off Bart O'Malley. The mare's racing name was Lear Jet, so Georgie had shortened it to Jet. She was an extremely edgy mare and as Georgie mounted up, Jet was so anxious her flanks were trembling.

"Easy, Jet," Georgie reassured her as she asked the mare to walk on.

Talking softly to the mare, Georgie walked her back and forth up and down the corridor as the other girls tacked up. She had almost got Jet calmed down, when she made the fatal mistake of leaning over the polo mallet stand and reaching in to grab herself a mallet. At the sight of the bamboo stick in her rider's hand Jet assumed she was in for a beating. Before Georgie could stop her, she had backed away in a total panic and kept on backing up all the way down the corridor!

"Jet!"

Georgie kicked the mare forward, trying once again, but Alice shook her head. "You won't get her near that stand. She thinks the polo stick is a whip."

Georgie dismounted and led the mare forward, but

as soon as she took a stick in her hand the whites of the mare's eyes showed and she backed away in a frenzy once more.

"She's not going to make much of a polo mare if I can't hold a stick anywhere near her!" Georgie was frustrated.

"Forget about the stick today," Alice suggested. "Just ride her without one."

Admitting defeat, Georgie rode Jet without a mallet out on to the polo fields. At least the mare had a nice canter, she thought as she urged her on to ride in a steady circle. Jet's ewe neck meant that she tended to run like a giraffe with her head held high, but Georgie eventually got her going nicely on the bit, cantering in a good, steady circle.

Emily emerged from the stables on her first mount of the day – one of the two chestnuts she had bought at Keeneland Park.

"They're easy to tell apart," Emily told Georgie. "Nala has a white coronet on her near hind and Jocasta hasn't got any white at all."

Emily was riding Jocasta first. The chestnut mare

seemed fine as she cantered her around on her own. She didn't even mind having the polo stick swinging alongside her. The problem came when Emily tried to ride the mare alongside Georgie and Jet. As soon as Jocasta pulled up alongside another horse, she fancied that she was in a race. Instead of turning when they reached the ball, Jocasta leaned against the bit and broke into a gallop. It took Emily a whole lap of the field to slow her down to a trot again and by then Jocasta had a lather of white sweat on her neck and her flanks were heaving. Emily was unperturbed. She had nerves of steel when it came to riding. She often told stories about life back home in New Zealand, most of which seemed to involve riding bareback at a gallop down the beach on young horses that had barely been broken. Being on a strung-out polo pony didn't worry Emily in the least. But Emily wasn't an aggressive rider and Georgie was concerned that her natural reticence might count against her on the field and make her stand back from tackling the other team.

Daisy didn't have that problem. In fact she was almost the opposite. She was so fiercely competitive that as soon as she was on the field she was in attack mode. Riding her bay Thoroughbred Francine, she hardly spent any time warming the mare up before she was practising her shoulder barges, cantering alongside Georgie and yanking on the reins to veer Francine hard to the left so that the horses rebounded off each other's shoulders like bumper cars.

At one point, Daisy and Francine nearly unseated Georgie with a shoulder barge that came out of nowhere.

"Hey!" Georgie shouted out to her. "What do you think you're doing?"

Daisy shrugged. "I've read the rule book and you're totally allowed to barge into the other rider – as long as the horses are directly side by side and you don't cut the other rider off."

Alice, meanwhile, had tacked up Marco the chestnut gelding and was giving him his first run. Not wasting any time, she took him straight out on to the field and urged him into a fast canter down the long side. She was charging down on a ball with her mallet raised, ready to swing when Marco pulled up suddenly without warning, doing a 180-degree turn on the spot. Alice, who hadn't been expecting the dramatic change of direction, was flung forward out of the saddle and lost her seat.

It was the first time that any of the girls had seen Alice even come close to falling off. She catapulted straight on to Marco's neck and had to cling on to stay onboard. Her face was completely white with shock by the time Georgie and the others reached her.

"Did you see that?" Alice said. "He's totally nuts!"

"I guess that's why the jockeys called him Spinner," Daisy pointed out.

By late afternoon, the girls had worked their way through all the Thoroughbreds that they'd bought at Keeneland Park, some with more success than others. Marco was quickly proving to be a nightmare. His habit of spinning round whenever something upset him was proving to be lethal.

"He's terrified of the ball! He's almost thrown me at least three times today," Alice groaned as she unsaddled.

The ponies had worked up a sweat in their first training session and after they untacked their last mounts, the girls took all seven horses to the hose-down bay to wash them down.

There was a notice above the wash bay – clearly installed recently – stating that riders must muck out their stalls every day and keep group areas tidy.

"Do you think it's a dig at us?" Emily asked as she washed down Jocasta and Nala. "Those Burghley House boys seem pretty sniffy about having to share their stable quarters."

"There's nothing they can do about it," Alice said. "Mrs Dickins-Thomson said we're allowed to be here."

"Still," Georgie said, "I wouldn't put it past Heath Brompton to try and get us kicked out for being untidy tenants."

"Then we'd better make sure he has nothing to complain about," Alice agreed.

They spent ages that afternoon cleaning the yard, mucking out the stalls and sorting their tack neatly on the racks in the storage room. By the time the girls had fed the mares and put them away in the stables, the dirt and sweat that had previously been on the horses had managed to transfer itself on to them instead. They were filthy, smelly and utterly exhausted. Georgie's jodhpurs were covered in dung and muck. She had the world's worst helmet hair and she'd been riding so hard her muscles ached.

"I can't wait to get back to the house," Alice said as they walked down the driveway together. "All I want to do is have a shower, eat dinner and collapse on the sofa and watch a movie—"

"Ohmygod!" Georgie suddenly froze in the middle of the school driveway.

"Ohmygod what?" Alice frowned.

"I forgot," Georgie winced. "I mean I totally forgot!"

The other girls looked at her expectantly.

"I've got a date," Georgie groaned.

It was 6pm on a Sunday night and right now, James Kirkwood was standing on the doorstep waiting to take her to the movies.

Chapter Nine

*G*eorgie had never actually been on a proper date before, but she was pretty sure that this wasn't how they were supposed to begin. She'd stormed past James on the step, muttering her apologies for being so late, too scared to actually slow down and talk to him in case he caught a whiff of the horse dung and sweat.

She would have understood if he'd given up on her after that, but he'd waited while she hastily showered, dressed and tried to resurrect her desperately bad helmet hair. Then they had caught the bus into Lexington in a mad rush and only just made it into the movie theatre in time.

The Lexington Lido was one of those old-fashioned cinemas with plush velvet seats and heavy curtains that pulled back from the screen as the movie started.

The movie was so old that it crackled and scratched on the screen as it played, but Georgie didn't care. She was consumed by the story. It was all about an English girl about her own age, whose name was Velvet. She was training a racehorse to win the Grand National. Even though some parts of the race itself looked a bit fake, the girl in the movie could ride really well – and her horse was gorgeous!

"Do you think it was really her?" Georgie asked James as they left the theatre afterwards. "You know, did the actress who played Velvet actually ride?"

James nodded. "Elizabeth Taylor did all her own stunts."

"Now that would be a cool job," Georgie said. "I would love to be a stunt double."

"I thought you wanted to be an eventer?" James said.

"I do," Georgie said. "And a part-time stunt rider."

"And a polo player?"

"You make me sound like I can't make up my mind," Georgie said.

"And you think you can?" James said. There was an edge to his voice as if he wasn't exactly joking.

Georgie frowned. "I get the feeling we're not talking about careers day any more?"

James raked a hand through his blond hair. "I'm just wondering if you know what you want, Georgie. And I'm wondering why this Riley keeps turning up. He's not even a polo player."

"Riley has contacts at Keeneland Park racetrack. He got us in so we could buy the horses," Georgie explained. "He was just trying to help."

"Well if you need any help from now on, you ask me, OK?" James said. "I don't want Riley hanging around Blainford."

They were almost back to the bus depot when Georgie spotted a massive poster on the wall of the town hall that featured the graphic blue silhouette of a horse galloping. The poster said: **Lexington Bluegrass Cup, February 10-11.**

"What's the Bluegrass Cup?" Georgie asked. "Is it some kind of race?"

James shook his head. "It's a polo tournament. Lots

of the major high-goal players travel to Lexington to play in it. The school usually lets us have a day pass to go and watch."

He looked meaningfully at Georgie. "I can get us tickets to one of the Patron's marquees, if you like."

"OK, " Georgie was staring at the poster oblivious to James' flirtations, "but I don't really care where I sit – and the girls will want to come too. Let's just sit with the school in the stands and then we can get Cam and Alex and JP along as well."

"Georgie," James took her hand and drew her attention away from the poster at last, "I have something for you."

He put his hand in his pocket, drew out a box and passed it to her.

"What's this?"

"Open it and find out."

Inside the box was a silver ring with the Blainford crest on it and a pale blue stone in the centre.

"It's my polo ring," James said. "I won it in the Burghley-Luhmuhlen match. The blue stone is the colour of Burghley House and it has my name inscribed on the back of it."

"It's really cool." Georgie passed the ring back to him.

"No," James said. "It's for you. I want you to wear it."

"You want me to have your polo ring?"

"Of course," James said, as he slipped it on Georgie's finger. "You're my girl, aren't you?"

✳

Georgie carried the ring in her pocket around school the next morning.

"Why aren't you wearing it?" Daisy asked as they sat down to lunch with Alice and Emily.

"I thought it was against the school rules to wear jewellery," Georgie said weakly. The truth was, the ring didn't feel right on her finger.

"Can I try it on?" Alice asked as she sat down with her lunch tray.

Georgie dug the ring out of her pocket and put it down on the table, but before Alice could lay a hand on it Emily had swooped it up. "MY precious!" she hissed when Alice tried to take it off her.

"Oh, for God's sake, Gollum! Give it here!" Alice examined the ring and slipped it on to her finger to admire it.

"It's not as glam as the one Wills gave to Kate," Daisy said, "but I guess it's OK."

"It's not an engagement ring," Georgie said.

"Well it sounds like he thinks so…" Daisy said.

"…which makes Kennedy your sister-in-law," Alice added.

"And on that cheery note," Georgie stood up and snatched her ring from between Alice's fingers, "I am going to go to polo class."

"Are we still meeting you after school at the stables for stick-and-ball?" Alice shouted after her. "Or will you be too busy making plans for your royal wedding?"

Georgie wished she felt as excited as her friends did about the polo ring, but she kept thinking about Riley.

When James dropped her back at Badminton House after the movie he had leaned in close to kiss her and Georgie actually found herself flinching! She made excuses about being seen by the housemistress, then ducked inside, closing the door on him. It felt like she was betraying Riley, being out with James – which was totally crazy! Georgie couldn't wait to get out on the polo field and clear her head.

She had decided to ride Belle again for Heath Brompton's class that afternoon. The polo master already had it in for her, so it was probably best if she didn't turn up on one of the new green Thoroughbreds.

As Georgie rode across the polo fields she noticed that the class was bigger than usual. When she got closer she realised that there were senior riders mixed in amongst her usual classmates. She felt a knot tighten in her stomach as she saw that one of the seniors was Conrad Miller.

"I'm merging three of my classes today," Heath Brompton explained to the students. "As you know, the Blainford Round Robin begins next week and I thought this would be a good opportunity to get some chukkas under your belts."

Heath Brompton surveyed his riders. "There should be enough riders here for two teams from each boarding house. I'll leave it to you to sort it out amongst yourselves, and allocate shirt numbers."

Heath Brompton frowned at Georgie. "Parker, you've got no team so I guess you're on the sidelines."

"Actually, sir," Georgie said, "I'm going to be playing in the Round Robin."

"So where are the rest of your team mates?"

"They don't take polo as an option subject – they're in the eventing class," Georgie explained, "but we've got permission to enter a Badminton House team. I thought the headmistress would have spoken to you about it by now?"

Heath frowned. It was clearly news to him, but he didn't want to let the students know that the headmistress had gone over his head and granted permission.

"Of course I know about it, Parker," he harrumphed. "You can join Luhmuhlen today – they need an extra player. We're playing King of the Field. The rules are pretty basic. If you win, then you stay on."

He turned to the polo class. "Right, let's have my boys from Burghley House up first, shall we?"

The first two teams on the field were both from Burghley House. Conrad was leading one of the teams wearing the number three shirt and Georgie had to admit that even though she couldn't stand him, he was a good player. Every time the ball shot free from the pack it was Conrad who got to it first. He had perfect timing at the gallop and an accurate swing, but the rest of his team mates weren't up to the same standard and a lot of the play was choppy and messy. There was a lot of mad galloping up and down the field, but very little in the way of goal-scoring. In the end, the only two goals were both scored by Conrad. His team stayed on the field to face the next challengers.

Heath Brompton blew his whistle. "Luhmuhlen? You're up next!"

"Hey, Parker," Conrad gave her a malicious grin as she rode past him to take her place on the field. He made a gesture as if slitting his throat. "You're mine."

It wasn't a hollow threat. From the moment that Heath Brompton threw the ball in, Georgie spent most of the game simultaneously trying to get her mallet on it and do her best to keep out of Conrad's way. But wherever she was, Burghley House's head prefect was right behind her.

Every time Georgie tried to make a play for the ball, Conrad would maliciously ride her off the line. One minute into play, she had the ball and suddenly Belle was reeling sideways as Conrad shoulder-barged his mare into her flank.

JP was right beside her and he pulled his mare up and raised his stick in the air to appeal to Mr Brompton. "Foul, sir! Conrad deliberately rode into her from behind!"

Heath Brompton blew his whistle. "No foul! Play on!"

The scores were tied at nil all and they were three minutes into the chukka when JP broke loose to make the first promising run for Luhmuhlen. Georgie rode Belle alongside him, in case he needed to pass the ball to her. She was focusing so hard on following the ball that the body blow from Conrad took her totally by surprise. Conrad had ridden up and cut right in front of her, using his mare's shoulder to block Georgie in. It was a totally illegal, dangerous move, but he clearly didn't care. Forcing Georgie to a stop, he took a second charge at her, ignoring the polo ball entirely as he slammed his mare into hers, body-checking her with his shoulder at the same time.

The unexpected impact flung Georgie sideways out of the saddle, but Belle moved to stay underneath her, so that Georgie was able to grasp at the neck strap where the martingale connected to the saddle and cling on long enough to get herself back upright again.

By the time she was aware of what Conrad had actually done to her, the Burghley prefect was long gone, up ahead of the rest of the players, chasing the ball and acting as if he hadn't just tried to intentionally push her off her horse.

Heath Brompton hadn't seen the foul so Georgie had no choice but to pull herself together and get back into the game. The Burghley team had just made it one-nil and this time it was Luhmuhlen's ball. JP took the opening shot and struck it straight to Georgie who tore off with it up the field. She could hear the hooves of the pack thundering behind her as she took a forehand shot to steer the ball towards the goal. The pack were gaining on her. This time she was on the alert for an attack from Conrad and as he went in for another shoulder charge she pulled Belle up abruptly and knee-barged him this time, riding him off his line. Conrad squealed like a stuck pig and threw up a stick in the air to cry foul. "Ref! She tried to eye-gouge me!"

The referee's whistle went. "Foul. Penalty to Burghley!"

Georgie couldn't believe it. "You have got to be kidding me! I didn't do anything!"

Heath Brompton's mouth became a thin line. "That's a foul by you against Miller, Parker. Step back into line and let him take the shot."

Georgie was trembling with suppressed rage as she took up her position with her team mates and was forced to watch as Conrad scored a penalty against them straight between the posts.

There was just one minute left in the chukka as Georgie took up her position ready for Heath Brompton's throw-in.

The ball was picked up quickly by the Luhmuhlen team. JP had the lead and the others were chasing him down the field. Georgie leaned forward over Belle's neck and as the mare got closer to the action, she manoeuvred to swing back with her mallet. She felt a snag as her stick caught in mid-air and then she glanced back over her shoulder just in time to see Conrad. He had hooked her stick with his own and in one deft move he grasped Georgie's polo stick in his other hand and pulled his mare up as he gave the stick a firm tug.

The sudden, violent yank on the other end of her stick was enough to throw Georgie's balance completely. She lost her stirrups and found herself plummeting straight down to the ground beneath the hooves of the ponies. She was on the field right in the middle of the pack and there was nothing she could do to avoid being trampled apart from curling into a ball, hands wrapped tight over her helmet. She felt a hoof catch her sharply on her right arm and then the pack had cleared and the next thing she knew JP was down on the ground by her side helping her up.

"Are you OK?"

Georgie was shaking with shock. She nodded. "I'm fine."

Heath Brompton was running across the field towards them. He had a worried look on his face. "Parker, are you all right?"

"I'm fine, sir."

"What happened?"

"Conrad hooked my stick and pulled me out of the saddle."

Heath Brompton looked shocked. "Is that what happened here, Miller?"

"No, sir," Conrad shook his head with an expression of pure innocence. "I did hook her stick, but it was an accident and I let go straight away. The real problem is that Parker got her reins tangled in her mare's mane and muddled herself up."

Georgie couldn't believe it. "That isn't what happened, sir! He did it on purpose! He pulled me off my horse!"

Heath Brompton's already well-grooved brow took on some new furrows as he appeared to consider the possibility of Conrad's guilt. But if he had any doubts about Burghley House's star player he soon dismissed them.

"Parker," Heath Brompton took her polo mallet from her, "I think you'd better take your mare back to the stables."

"But, sir," Georgie protested, "it wasn't—"

"Parker!" The polo master was adamant. "Go now

– and while you're there, hog her stupid mane like I told you to do last week!"

✳

By the time Georgie had reached the stables she was in tears. The shock of the fall had made her start to weep, but it was the unfairness of it all that kept her crying. She hated the way Conrad had the trust of the teachers just because he was a senior. He was always going to get away with it. And now, once again Heath Brompton thought of her as a liability. The look on his face made it clear that he wished she didn't exist.

Georgie had undone Belle's tack and sponged the mare down. She was just sorting out her feed when the girls arrived for practice.

"What happened to you?" Alice asked when she saw the grass stains on Georgie's jodhpurs.

"Conrad Miller," Georgie said. "He pulled me off my horse."

"You're kidding!" Emily was horrified.

"Do I look like I'm in the mood for jokes?" Georgie

asked as she marched back across the corridor with Belle's feed.

"Are you OK?" Daisy asked. "I mean, can you still ride? Do you want to have stick-and-ball with us, because it's OK if you don't."

"Oh, I'm riding!" Georgie said through gritted teeth. "We need to get those mares trained up if we're taking on Conrad in the Round Robin."

She turned to Alice. "Could you do me a favour and saddle Marco up for me? There's something I need to do before we ride."

While the others went to get the horses ready Georgie went to the tack shed and hunted around in the recesses beneath the grooming kits. When she found what she was looking for she returned to Belle's stall. She plugged the clippers into the power socket in the wall and stood there mesmerised by the whirring vibrations. Then she walked over to Belle and grasped a thick hank of the mare's lustrous jet-black mane and began to shave.

Chunks of mane fell to the floor as she ran the clippers up the mare's neck. Georgie looked at the beautiful black mane lying on the floor, but felt no remorse. All she felt right now was a grim determination to see this through to the end. If Conrad thought he could terrorise her and push her around then he was wrong. She would meet him on the polo field and next time she would play it her way. Next time she would win.

Chapter Ten

*B*elle's mane was gone and all that was left was a hedgehog stump of black hair that ran along the crest of the mare's neck.

She looks like a different horse, Georgie thought. She didn't even look like a mare any more, the girlish prettiness had somehow vanished and all that remained was the bare, brutal anatomy of her neck, the hard outline of her shoulders and withers.

"Wow!" Alice leaned over the door of the loose box. "You actually did it."

Georgie was still staring at her, shocked by the transformation. "She looks naked."

"She looks like a warrior," Alice said. She smiled at

Georgie. "Come on, while you've got the clippers out – let's do them all."

Hogging off Belle's mane had been hard for Georgie, but there was a sense of excitement in the task as they worked their way through all the horses together.

Daisy and Emily got another set of clippers out of the tack room and they worked in two teams. By the end of the hogging session there was a huge pile of black and chestnut hair on the floor.

"If we glued it all together we could make a miniature pony," Emily suggested. Her sense of humour failed though when the time came to cut into Barclay's mane.

"Are you sure you're OK?" Daisy said when she saw the look on Emily's face.

"I'm fine," Emily insisted. "Just get it over with!" She had held the big black horse steady as Daisy ran the clippers up the crest, but when Daisy had almost reached Barclay's ears Emily suddenly yelled, "Wait!"

She reached out and took hold of the last hank of mane up by his bridlepath.

"OK, cut now."

As Daisy sheared through the mane, Emily kept the

hank of hair tight in her fist and then put it in her pocket.

Not all horses are willing to stand still for the clippers and predictably the worst was Marco. After nearly being stomped on and kicked by him several times, Georgie groaned, "I give up!"

"But he's half-hogged!" Alice said.

"Put a twitch on him," Emily suggested.

The twitch looked a bit like a torture device, but it was actually a very useful piece of kit. It was a wooden baton with a rope loop attached to the end of it. Within moments of the twitch being applied to his top lip, it was as if Marco had been sedated. He stood utterly relaxed as Alice took the clippers and finished the job.

"Good boy!" Georgie released the twitch and Marco gave his head a brisk shake, as if he was waking up from a hypnotist's trance.

The girls lined the sixteen horses up and admired their efforts.

"They look like a proper string now," Georgie said.

Alice looked at the drifts of horse mane piled ankle-deep on the floor. "Let's clean up," she said. "It's too late to train today, but tomorrow, after school, we play."

✳

Over the next week the Badminton House team really began to take shape. The girls met every day after school for stick-and-ball out on the playing field, working to Alice's roster, each riding four horses in a session.

After the first training session with Jet, Georgie had spent some extra time with the mare, at first just standing alongside her and holding the mallet, and then, once the mare seemed OK with that, taking its handle and stroking her all over with it to let her know that the mallet wasn't going to hurt her.

The first time she carried a mallet on Jet the mare was tense and jogged about anxiously, side-stepping every time Georgie tried to take a shot. By the second session on the polo field, Georgie was swinging the stick back and forth and Jet was cantering along without a care.

The Dupree ponies were far superior to the new Thoroughbreds. The best of them all was undoubtedly

Desiray. The little dun mare was a true polo pony, gutsy and tough.

According to Alice, if Desiray could talk she would have told you how thrilled she was to be making a comeback from her untimely retirement. When Alice tacked her up, Desiray would tremble with anticipation and by the time she reached the field she would be in a lather of white sweat from excitement before she even began to play. On the pony lines during her warm-up Desiray was prone to bouts of high-spirited bucking, but once she was on the field she was as focused and ruthless as her rider. She loved nothing better than to run another mare off the ball and would come shoulder-to-shoulder with her rival and then perform a neat shoulder charge to take possession without any cue whatsoever from her rider.

"She plays way better than I do," Alice said proudly.

Of the Dupree ponies, Daisy's favourite was Jada, a stocky and serious mare. But Daisy's absolute favourite turned out to be the little fifteen-hand bay, Francine, who she'd bought off the track at Keeneland.

Francine and Daisy both shared a love of speed and

a killer instinct for driving straight into the pack and swiping at anything that moved until they got to the ball.

When the pack were chasing the ball Emily often held back, but she was quickly developing into a smart tactical player with a very good arm for making long shots up the field. Her favourite mare was Vita, the pretty brown mare with the socks and white star, who was fit and sound and good at covering the ground quickly.

Despite having favourites, the girls tried to roster the ponies around so that everyone got a turn trying out each horse.

There was one pony on the roster however that no one was pleased to be given. Marco was a nightmare.

"Why have I been lumbered with Spinner again?" Daisy groaned on Friday when she saw that she had been rostered on to the chestnut gelding.

"His name is Marco," Georgie said.

"He will always be Spinner to me!" Daisy shot back. "And I'm not getting on him. Not after yesterday."

Yesterday's training had ended in total carnage after

Marco had done one of his famous 180-degree turns in mid-gallop with Daisy on his back. The turn had been so sudden and forceful that Daisy hadn't stood a chance of staying onboard. She had been violently catapulted out of the saddle. Which wasn't so bad, she told the others afterwards. It was the fact that Marco had then gone after her once she was on the ground.

Georgie wouldn't have believed it if she hadn't seen it herself. The horse had attacked Daisy, hooves flying as he tried to land a strike on her. It was only the swift intervention of the other girls driving him off that had stopped Marco from causing serious harm.

"I'm not getting on him." Daisy put her foot down. "I'm not a coward, but I'm not an idiot either – that horse is crazy."

"All right," Georgie had given in. "You take Jet for the last chukka. I'll ride Marco."

As they tacked up the ponies for the final chukka, Georgie kept an eye on Marco's legs and head. The gelding had been known to try and bite and kick simultaneously while he was being tacked up. Today, he made a desultory attempt to sink his teeth into

Georgie's arm as she tightened the girth, but she was able to brush him aside easily with a quick tap on the muzzle.

"Don't be naughty."

Marco seemed to take the telling-off to heart and stood still for the rest of the tacking up. But he clearly had revenge on his mind. It was two minutes into the chukka and Georgie had just won the ball off Alice and was racing for the goal when Marco did his legendary spinning trick. This time, he did the 180-degree turn, but when Georgie by some miracle managed to stay onboard, he didn't stop there.

She had been flung forward out of the saddle by the sudden stop-and-turn and, as she tried to get her stirrups back, she suddenly felt the horse give way underneath her. Marco's knees appeared to be collapsing!

"Georgie!" She heard Alice yelling at her. "Jump!"

Without thinking, Georgie obeyed on instinct. She threw herself off the horse and fell clear, just as Marco slumped completely beneath her, dropped down on his side and began to roll.

The girls watched helplessly as the gelding thrashed

back and forth. Georgie heard a loud crack as the tree that ran down the inside of the polo saddle was literally snapped in two. If she'd stayed onboard it could just as easily have been her spine snapping as Marco had crushed her beneath him.

With a look of triumph, having got rid of his rider and destroyed his saddle, the chestnut gelding stood up and shook himself with a satisfied grunt.

"What did I say?" Daisy helped Georgie to her feet. "That horse is a lunatic."

Georgie, still shaking from her forced dismount, couldn't disagree with her.

Marco was proving to be the worst purchase she had ever made. He would have to go. And she knew the only person who would possibly take him on.

"I'd better call Riley."

✳

Georgie had been glad of an excuse to call Riley. She hadn't spoken to him since they'd had that stupid fight. She was prepared for him to hang up on her, but he listened to what Georgie had to say, and seemed strangely unsurprised when Georgie told him about Marco's misdemeanours.

"It sounds like you've bought yourself some trouble," Riley said. "I'll take him off your hands if you want. I'll do you a straight trade. I've got a little grey mare here, one of my breakers, that might make you a good polo pony. She's built for it – good hindquarters and hocks, and she's a sweetheart to ride."

"She sounds great." Georgie was so relieved. She was even more stunned when Riley said. "I'll come by after school tomorrow and bring the mare and take Marco. Meet me at the stables at five."

"Thanks, Riley." Georgie couldn't believe he was bringing the mare to the school. She knew how much Riley hated having anything to do with Blainford. "I really appreciate it. I thought after the other day that you might not even speak to me…"

She stopped talking when she realised that there was no one at the other end of the phone. Riley had already hung up.

✳

The next day after school Riley arrived in the horse truck and the girls all gathered round to see the new pony. Georgie had told them that the mare was one of Riley's 'breakers' – a young, just-broken-in horse. Georgie hadn't been expecting much – a breaker was usually not long in from the wild, with a coarse coat, tangled mane and not much condition. But the grey mare that Riley brought out of the truck was the total opposite. She was a glossy dapple-grey, well-fed and rounded with a beautifully hogged mane and trimmed fetlocks. She had a handsome face with a very slight Roman nose and deep brown eyes that looked wise beyond her years.

"She's gorgeous!" Georgie couldn't believe it.

"She's a nice mare," Riley agreed.

"How old is she?" Georgie asked.

"Nearly five," Riley said. "Dad won her in a claiming race when she was just a yearling."

"What's that?" Georgie asked.

"It's a race where the winner can claim your horse," Riley explained. "Dad did a deal with one of the jockeys and somehow I ended up with her. She was too young to do anything so I turned her out to grow until she was three and then last year I started to break her in. I was planning to race her this season, but she'll make a good polo pony."

Georgie ran a hand over the mare's glossy dappled coat. She felt every bit as smooth and muscular as she looked. Her conformation was amazing, short-coupled just like a polo pony should be with a length of neck and good hard hooves.

"What's her name?" Georgie asked.

"Princess."

"No, really. What's her name?"

Riley shrugged. "I thought it suited her."

Georgie put her arm round the mare's neck. "What do you say, Princess? You want to stay here with us girls and learn to play polo?"

"She already knows a few polo moves," Riley confessed. "I've been training her up for the past week or so in the round pen at home. She's a quick learner."

Georgie couldn't believe it. Riley had even been schooling the mare for her? It was far too good to be true.

"Are you sure you want to trade her for Marco?" Georgie asked.

"Hey!" Alice interjected. "Don't discourage him!"

Riley grinned. "I'm sure," he said. "You have the mare. I'll take Marco."

"Come on," Alice said, "let's get him on the truck before Riley changes his mind."

Loading Marco was potentially a three-man job so Emily and Daisy both went out with Alice, leaving Riley and Georgie to put Princess in the loose box.

They put the mare into Marco's old stall, sliding the bolt across on the bottom Dutch door so that she could still look out into the corridor and see her new stable mates.

"So," Riley looked around uncomfortably, "I guess I better get going before the lord of the manor turns up and freaks out at me for talking to you like last time."

"He's not like that," Georgie said looking down at James's polo ring round her finger.

"Oh no, he's real friendly," Riley said sarcastically.

Riley shuffled about and hesitated for a moment and then he said, "Can I ask you something?"

"Sure, what?"

"You know what you were saying the other day, about how I didn't call you? Well, what if I had? If I'd called you after the Formal, do you think you'd still be going out with him... instead of me?"

"What?" Georgie felt confused. "Riley, I can't answer that. I don't know."

"Because the thing is," Riley continued, "if you want to know the truth, I've been wanting to call you every day since that dance."

"So why didn't you?"

Riley pulled a face. "Geez, Georgie, I don't know. It's this whole Blainford thing. I got home that night after the dance in my rented suit and I realised I was kidding myself. I don't belong here."

"But that doesn't matter," Georgie said. "I'm the one who goes to school here – not you."

"That's my point," Riley said. "You're supposed to be here. You and I, we're different."

"No," Georgie shook her head. "We're the same. You're a talented rider, Riley – you could be at this school on a scholarship if you weren't such a... snob."

"I'm a snob?"

"Yeah." Georgie was really winding into her argument now. "You're a reverse snob. You won't go out with me because I go to a good school. What's that about?"

"Well, that's about me being an idiot – obviously!" Riley shot back. "Because I thought after that dance that you were my girlfriend and then suddenly I find out you're going out with his majesty with the polo mallet."

"How can I go out with you if you never call me?" Georgie was astonished. "I thought you'd dumped me! And his name is James and he's really nice; you don't know him."

"But I know you," Riley said. "And I know that you shouldn't be with him. You should be with me!"

Alice suddenly appeared at the door. "Hey, Riley, we've got Marco on at last—" she stopped in mid-sentence when she saw the look on Georgie and Riley's faces.

"I can't talk about this any more," Riley said. He cast a sorrowful glance at Georgie and the grey mare. "So long, Princess," he said. "Take care."

✳

"Well, I'm glad to see the back of him!" Daisy said, dusting off her hands dramatically as she walked back into the stable block.

Georgie looked miserable.

"Daisy!" Alice said. "Try and have some tact!"

"What?" Daisy said. "I meant Spinner! Not Riley."

Daisy stuck her head over the loose-box door and took a good, hard look at Princess.

"That's quite a horse!" she said. "And Riley just swapped her for Spinner? What was he thinking?"

Alice looked sideways at Georgie, but didn't say anything.

"Shall we include Princess in the workout roster?" Emily asked. "The Round Robin knockout tournament is in two weeks. That doesn't give us much time to start training her."

"Let's give her today to settle in first," Georgie said. "I'll hog her mane and start her off on some stick-and-ball tomorrow."

While the others went off to get their training session underway, Georgie mixed Princess a feed.

Marco had always been vicious at feeding time and

you had to keep a careful eye on him in case he attacked you. But Georgie could see that Princess wasn't like that. The mare had a gentleness about the eyes that made Georgie trust her. She slipped the feed bin into the rack on the wall and then stood beside the mare as she ate.

As she stood there in the loose box she looked down at the polo ring on her finger. She'd got it covered in sugarbeet when she was mixing the horse feed. She slipped it off and wiped it on her shirt.

The ring hadn't even been on her finger long enough to leave a mark. It was as if she had never worn it. She stared at the ring for a moment longer and then, as if coming to a decision, she put it in her pocket and went to tack up Belle.

Chapter Eleven

*A*t boarding school, trying to avoid someone was almost impossible. So why was it that when Georgie actually wanted to run into James Kirkwood he was nowhere to be seen? On Sunday night she'd lingered at the dining hall, taking ages to eat her dessert, just in case he turned up late. Then she'd dawdled on the driveway as the girls walked past Burghley House, walking as slowly as humanly possible, but still he didn't appear.

Georgie knew she wouldn't run into him on Monday morning since James was a year ahead of her and not in any of her classes. It wasn't until the afternoon when she was at the Burghley House stables getting Princess ready for her polo lesson that she finally saw him.

With the Round Robin less than two weeks away she

needed to launch into Princess's training straight away. She needed to try the mare out on the field to get a sense of her ability.

Georgie had done up her tendon boots and was just finishing off an Argie knot on Princess's tail when she had that strange feeling you get when you're being watched. She looked up and started in surprise when she saw James leaning over the Dutch door, smiling at her.

"Ohmygod, you scared me!" Georgie said.

"Did I?" James asked.

Georgie returned to her tail plaiting. "So where have you been?" she asked. "I didn't see you at dinner last night."

"I got a last-minute pass out," James said. "Dad flew in from New York – he took Kennedy and me out for a family dinner."

"Nice."

"Anything is better than the dining hall," James said airily.

He cast an eye over the grey mare in the stall.

"Got a new horse?"

Georgie nodded. "Her name's Princess."

She finished the tail plait and then did three neat twists, like a chignon, before tying off the ends so that the tail was tucked up.

"She's a good-looking mare. Where did you get her from?"

Georgie had known that this would be his next question. And she also knew that James wasn't going to like the answer.

"I exchanged one of my other horses for her."

James frowned. "What do you mean?"

"I swapped horses with Riley. He took Marco and he gave me Princess."

"This mare is Riley's horse?"

"Well, not technically," Georgie said. "She's mine now. We traded."

"I thought you told me that you weren't seeing him any more." James's tone had turned defensive.

Georgie shook her head. "You said you didn't want me to see him. I never agreed."

"So you're hanging out with him behind my back? He's been here again, in these stables, after I told him to stay away?"

"You don't actually have the right to order him off school property, James," Georgie replied. "It's not like you own Blainford."

"We own quite a lot of it. My family paid for the library," James countered.

"Well the next time Riley comes round I'll make sure he doesn't borrow any books," Georgie said.

"Is that supposed to be a joke?" James said. "There's not going to be a next time, Georgie. I don't want you seeing him."

"James," Georgie said, "is this really about Riley? Or is it about you owning me like you own the library and everything else around here?"

"What are you talking about?" James's eyes blazed with anger.

Georgie knew it was too late to back down now. "The other day, when you asked me out, was it because you really wanted to go to the movies with me or were you just trying to outdo JP?"

James frowned. "You think I'm going out with you just to mess with JP?"

"No," Georgie said, "I think you asked me out to

mess with JP and then you gave me that ring because you were jealous of me and Riley."

Georgie reached into her pocket and pulled out the polo ring. "Here – I want you to take it back."

She handed him the ring and watched as James closed his fist round it until his knuckles turned white. "So that's it? You're dumping me for some loser who doesn't even go to Blainford?"

"It's not just because of Riley," Georgie said. "I don't think we should ever have got back together. Things have been weird between us."

James glared at her. "You are so ungrateful. I take you back, despite everything you've done. And now you do this? Kennedy was right – you're not good enough to date a Kirkwood!"

"Hang on a minute!" Georgie's eyes widened. "You dumped me because you were too stupid to realise your own sister was pulling your strings. Then you wanted me back – but only because you were jealous of JP and Riley. And now you're upset because my dumping you is going to make you look bad? Oh, and do tell me again about how special the

Kirkwoods are – I never get tired of hearing about that!"

Georgie grabbed Princess by the reins and unbolted the door to the loose box, but James blocked her way.

"Georgie, you don't want to do this. If you get on the wrong side of me I have the power to make your life hell at this school."

Georgie laughed. "Make it hell? Where have you been for the past term?"

She pushed past him, led Princess out of the loose box and mounted up. As she trotted the mare down the corridor she suddenly felt very glad that she was on her way to play polo. She had never felt quite so much like hitting something before in her life.

✳

Georgie was running late and she was still shaken from her fight with James when she arrived at polo class.

"Are you all right?" JP muttered to her.

"I'm fine," she told him. "I'll tell you about it later."

"We're having a proper match today," Heath

Brompton told the class. "We'll split into four teams and use two fields."

Georgie raised a hand. "Sir, can I be excused from the teams? Is it all right if I just play stick-and-ball by myself up the sidelines?"

Georgie would have loved to have joined in the game to let off steam, but she knew it was the wrong thing to do. Princess had never played polo before and Georgie had to ease her into the game gently.

And so she looked on enviously while the other riders played proper chukkas on the main fields and she kept Princess on the sidelines, working her back and forth, getting her accustomed to being near the mallet and the polo ball, and testing her speed and responses.

As she left the field Heath Brompton barked at her, "If you can't take the heat, Parker, perhaps you should consider getting out of the kitchen."

It wasn't until she was untacking Princess that Georgie finally twigged what he meant.

"Heath thinks I skipped the game because I'm scared of falling off again!" Georgie told the others when they met for stick-and-ball after school. "So now he thinks I'm a coward!"

As if to make up for it, Georgie played fast and furious in the stick-and-ball session that afternoon. The girls were training in earnest now and all sixteen ponies were given a workout. After over an hour of nonstop charging up and down the field on different ponies Georgie was exhausted. As they walked back down the driveway to the boarding house that evening she felt like her legs were going to buckle underneath her.

Back at Badminton House she collapsed on her bed. "I can't move."

"We have to move," Alice groaned. "We have to get dressed and go to dinner."

"I'm not going," Georgie said.

"Because you're too tired?"

"No. Because I've just split up with James and if I go to the dining hall I'm bound to see him."

"You've what?" Alice sat bolt upright again on her bed. "When did this happen?"

"Just before polo class. I was going to tell you, but I didn't want to make a big scene in front of the others."

"Was it an ugly break-up?" Alice asked. "Or are you still friends?"

"If by friends you mean has he threatened to ruin my life and make me miserable for all eternity at Blainford, then yeah," Georgie replied, "we're still friends."

"So you're never eating again?"

"Can you smuggle me back some food?"

"Georgie! It's lasagne night. Where am I going to put it? In my pockets? Pull yourself together and let's go."

From the moment Georgie walked into the dining hall the murmur rose up from the Burghley House table. She heard her name being called across the dining room by boys she didn't even know, but she didn't turn round. She didn't give them the satisfaction of looking at them when she got pelted on the back of the head with peas throughout the dinner.

"Just ignore them," Alice said sympathetically. Daisy and Emily banded round her for support as they walked out of the dining hall and stayed by her side, ignoring the taunts that followed them all the way down the driveway.

James had already succeeded in turning the whole of Burghley House against her.

✳

For the rest of the week, James and the Burghley boys didn't ease off on their hate campaign against Georgie. There wasn't a meal in the dining room that didn't end with her picking food out of her hair. The infamous seagull squawks – a Burghley hazing tradition – became a constant as the girls walked home each night.

"You should tell the headmistress," Emily said.

"Tell her what, Emily?" Georgie groaned. "That a boy is picking on me? That's exactly what he wants me to do."

Far better, Georgie thought, to suffer in silence. And James wasn't the only thing making her unhappy – she still desperately missed Tara Kelly's classes. Alice, Emily and Daisy were super-tactful around her and tried not to talk about cross-country at all, but now and then they would forget and let slip a bit of gossip about what sort of fences they were jumping or who was at the top of the class rankings. Disturbingly, Georgie kept hearing

Kennedy Kirkwood's name being mentioned in the same breath as 'clear round'. It was too awful to think that the girl who got her kicked out of class might now be dominating the rankings.

On Thursday Georgie arrived at her first class of the morning to find Daisy, Emily and Alice poring over the notice board in the quad.

"They've posted the teams for the Round Robin Knockout next weekend," Daisy said.

"Georgie," Emily said. "Before you look at it you have to promise that you won't get upset."

"Why would I get upset?" Georgie frowned.

"Because we're playing a Burghley House team…" Emily said, "… and James Kirkwood is in it."

Georgie groaned. "Well at least my life can't possibly get any worse."

"Yes, it can," Daisy said. "Conrad is in the team too."

✳

Strangely enough, knowing that they were playing against Burghley actually cheered Georgie up. The polo field was the perfect place for some very public revenge.

If James thought that Georgie's breaking up with him was embarrassing, just wait until she smeared the polo field with him!

All the girls were determined to beat the Burghley House boys and prove that Badminton House deserved to have a polo team. They had been riding for two hours every day after school and some nights Georgie's legs ached so much that she could barely walk up the driveway for dinner. Alice remained the stand-out player on the team, but everyone had raised their game. Emily had become adept at her long shots and taking the ball swiftly up the sidelines – which made her a natural in the number four position. Daisy stayed at number one, upfront where she could take shots at goal. She had biceps like a rock by now and she never gave away any ground to the opposition no matter what. Alice was in the coveted number three jersey and Georgie was in a roaming position at number two.

What the girls really needed though was some actual real game experience and it was Emily who suggested a friendly match against Luhmuhlen.

"Your team needs some proper play before the

competition," Emily said to Alex at breakfast, "and so do we. We could treat it like a real game. Four full chukkas. Just like the Round Robin."

"We can have the friendly game after school on Friday," Alice added. "Then rest the ponies on the Saturday before the real Round Robin begins on Sunday."

"Sounds great," JP agreed.

Cameron was more cautious with his enthusiasm. "OK, but you need to be aware that we're treating this just like a proper match. We can't go easy on you girls."

"Yeah," Alex agreed. "The other boys aren't going to cut you any slack on the field when the real games begin so it wouldn't be fair if we let you get away with stuff. Don't expect us to stop play just because you've broken a nail or something."

"Gotcha," Alice stifled a laugh. "No special treatment."

✳

The 'friendly' match between Luhmuhlen and Badminton was carnage. But not the sort that the boys had anticipated. It was seven-nil to the girls by the end of the third chukka. Alex and Cameron didn't know what had hit them.

"Can you tell your girlfriend to be a bit more careful?" Cameron whined to Alex as they mounted up on their fourth ponies to end the match. "She knee-barged and caught me square on the thigh!"

"If you ladies could possibly pull yourselves together to play the last chukka," JP groaned, "then at least we can potentially save ourselves the supreme embarrassment of losing without any points on the board?"

"Plus the embarrassment of Tara Kelly watching as we lose," Alex added, pointing out the dark-haired figure standing on the sidelines.

Tara had been watching the match since the first chukka began, but as the riders were about to take to the field for the fourth and final round she wrapped her coat round her and walked off the fields.

Georgie hadn't noticed Tara's presence on the sidelines. She was far too focused on the game. She had been playing brilliantly and two of the seven goals so far were hers. For the final chukka she was riding

Princess, who was fast becoming her favourite polo pony. She had been the last to finish tacking up, and the others were waiting to start play as she rode the dapple-grey mare on to the field to take up her position.

At the throw-in it was Luhmuhlen's ball, but the boys managed to lose possession almost straight away as Alice rode aggressively into the pack and stole it from JP, making a clean drive down the wing to Georgie.

There was a thundering of hooves alongside Georgie and she knew other riders were on her tail. Without looking back, she did the safest thing she could, hitting the ball swiftly and cleanly across the field to where Daisy could receive it and continue on towards the goal.

The shot she made was a good one, but for some reason Daisy didn't chase down the ball. Instead, she pulled her mare up and began waving her hands at Georgie across the field, shouting to her.

Georgie couldn't hear what Daisy was saying. Behind her, the hooves were still pounding loudly, which was odd since she'd offloaded the ball. Shouldn't the pack be heading towards Daisy instead of her?

Georgie realised too late why Daisy was shouting at

her. She turned just in time to see two riders bearing down on her with their mallets raised. There was nothing so unusual about that – except that these two riders weren't the ones she was playing against. It was Conrad, with James Kirkwood riding behind him. By the time she saw them there was nothing she could do. Conrad's mare came in slamming hard against Princess's right flank, and he put out his arm and gave Georgie a violent shove. Before she could do anything to save herself the ground was rushing up to meet her.

Chapter Twelve

*T*he body blow had come out of nowhere and Georgie didn't have the chance to prepare herself before she hit the ground. She landed badly on her right side, getting the wind knocked out of her as she impacted, gasping for air.

As she struggled back on her feet, feeling decidedly wobbly, she couldn't believe what had just happened. She had never been blindsided like that before and the experience had left her shaken – her face was white with shock.

"Are you OK?" Alice was the first to reach her.

"I'm fine," Georgie insisted. Her arm ached a little and she noticed a trickle of blood from her elbow next to a rip in her blouse. It was only a small graze, and nothing seemed to be broken. She was still surprisingly wobbly though and as she tried to take a step forward she felt her legs give way underneath her.

"It's delayed shock from the fall," Alice said. "Conrad really took you out."

She leapt down and helped Georgie over to the sideboards at the edge of the field. "Sit here and take deep breaths," Alice said, bending over Georgie, who was still pale and shaken and having trouble breathing as Daisy and Emily joined them.

Daisy was leading Princess. "Conrad has gone too far this time," she said. "He could have killed you! He actually pushed you off your horse!"

"He's a psychopath!" Emily agreed. "And what about James? He just watched him do it and he didn't even try to stop him!"

"The boys rode after them," Daisy added, "but it's not like they can do anything. Conrad is, like, twice their size and a prefect."

Georgie took a deep breath and pushed herself up off the ground.

"Hey, maybe you should wait before you try and get

up," Alice cautioned. But Georgie ignored her. She stood up and brushed the dirt off her jods. "Can you look after my horse for me?" she asked Alice.

"Sure, but where are you going?"

"Conrad has got to be stopped," Georgie said. "I'm going to see the headmistress."

✳

Mrs Dickins-Thomson was in the process of packing up her desk for the weekend when Georgie knocked at the door.

"Enter!" the headmistress said briskly.

"Mrs Dickins-Thomson?" Georgie stuck her head in the door. "I know it's late. I'm sorry to bother you."

"Nonsense, Miss Parker." The headmistress carried on with her paperwork. "I told you my door is always open. Come in."

When Mrs Dickins-Thomson caught sight of Georgie's ripped blouse, mud-stained jodhpurs and pale face she stopped shuffling papers at once.

"You've had an accident?"

"Well, sort of," Georgie said. "I was playing polo with

the Badminton House girls and Conrad Miller pushed me off my horse. It wasn't an accident though."

"You think he did it on purpose?" Mrs Dickins-Thomson was taken aback.

"Conrad has a major problem with me," Georgie explained. "It's the start of the Round Robin on Sunday and my team are scheduled to play against Burghley House – that's Conrad's team."

"And you're concerned that if you play against Burghley there's going to be a repeat of today's incident," Mrs Dickins-Thomson said.

Georgie nodded. "I don't think Conrad should be allowed to play," she said. "He's dangerous. He could have killed me out there."

"Miss Parker, you should have realised when you took up polo that there would be rough and tumble."

"But Conrad wasn't even supposed to be there. And he did it on purpose!"

Mrs Dickins-Thomson frowned. "Did a teacher witness this episode?"

Georgie shook her head. "No, just us."

"I'm afraid without a teacher to back you up, I can

hardly get Conrad Miller banned from the tournament," Mrs Dickins-Thomson said.

Georgie looked devastated.

"Well, can you at least have the Round Robin redrawn so that we're playing another team?" Georgie asked hopefully. "One that doesn't have Conrad in it?"

Mrs Dickins-Thomson considered this. "Sit down for a moment," she said to Georgie. She stood up from her desk and left Georgie alone in the office staring at the painting of Seabiscuit. When she returned a few minutes later the polo master was with her.

"I've been explaining your situation to Mr Brompton," Mrs Dickins-Thomson said. "He seems to think that the problem is a bit more deep-seated than just today's incident."

Heath Brompton nodded. "Georgie has been having problems holding her own on the polo field since the term began. She had a serious fall two weeks ago and then last week she refused to play a chukka because she was too nervous to go on the field. She stayed on the sidelines instead playing stick-and-ball by herself rather than joining her team and taking part in a game."

"Is that true Miss Parker?"

"Well, sort of," Georgie started. "But Conrad caused my fall that time too. He hooked my stick!"

"Falling is a part of playing polo, Miss Parker," Heath Brompton said. "I've already told you, I'm not entirely sure that someone of your –" he hesitated, choosing his words carefully – "sensibilities is suitable as a player. You can't expect to be treated differently."

"But I don't!" Georgie couldn't believe this was happening.

Mrs Dickins-Thomson frowned. "You say you aren't asking for special treatment, Georgie, but you've come in here asking me to change the Round Robin draw to your advantage. I can't exhibit favouritism towards the girls' team."

"They've been nothing but trouble as far as I'm concerned." Heath Brompton saw his chance. "We should never have allowed a girls' team in the tournament in the first place. It goes against the traditions of the academy."

Mrs Dickins-Thomson looked thoughtful. "I'm very keen to establish a girls' polo team, but I agree this is hardly an auspicious start. The board of the academy will be attending the polo on Sunday and I don't want their first glimpse of our new girls' team to be tears and tantrums on the field."

She turned to Georgie. "I think we've rushed you into this too quickly, Miss Parker. We've got your team up and running before they were ready for the cut and thrust of competition."

"What?" Georgie was confused. "No! It's not like that. We'll play Burghley!"

But it was too late to backtrack.

"I'm sorry, Miss Parker, but I am withdrawing the Badminton House girls' team from the Round Robin this year. Give yourselves a full season of training and then we can look at entering a girls' team in the tournament next year," Mrs Dickins-Thomson said.

"But that isn't what I meant to happen!" Georgie was horrified. "We've been training really hard. We're ready for this."

"Miss Parker, I'm afraid your actions tell a different story," Mrs Dickins-Thomson said. The stern tone of her voice made it clear that the conversation was over.

"There will be no girls' team in the Blainford Round Robin this year."

✳

When Georgie arrived back at Badminton House, the others were waiting in the living room for her.

"How did it go?" Emily said eagerly. "Is Conrad going to get his butt kicked?"

"Not exactly," Georgie admitted.

There was a stunned silence as she told the girls the whole story.

"I knew I should have come with you to back you up!" Alice was furious.

"Didn't you explain to her how Conrad did it on purpose?" Emily asked.

"I can understand them dropping you from the Round Robin, but how did you manage to take the rest of us down with you?" Daisy asked.

"Daisy!" Alice glared at her.

"Well?" Daisy shrugged. "I'd just like to know how it is that Georgie gets knocked off a horse and then suddenly I'm the one who's not playing in the tournament."

"None of us are playing, Daisy," Emily said. "Because we're a team. And a team of four – minus one – is no longer a team."

"It's not just about me," Georgie said. "Heath Brompton has this whole thing about girls playing. He thinks we're too soft to ride against the boys and my complaint was the perfect excuse for him to get us dropped from the competition."

"So what now?" Emily asked.

"We wait until next year, I guess," Georgie said.

"There has to be another way to get back in," Alice said, but for once none of the girls could think of an answer.

✳

It was Sunday morning straight after breakfast and the girls were walking down the driveway heading for Badminton House.

"The Round Robin starts in an hour," Georgie groaned. "I can't believe we're not in it!"

"Hey," Emily looked down the driveway at the red pick-up heading towards them, "is that Riley?"

Riley pulled up in front of the girls and wound down his window. "Hey, Georgie!"

"You're not allowed to drive up here," Georgie hissed at him. "It's out of bounds!"

"Oops!" Riley grinned. "Maybe one of the prefects will give me Fatigues."

"Riley! I'm serious!" Georgie was beginning to freak out. Everyone was looking at them. "You need special permission. If Conrad sees you he'll use it as an excuse to punish me."

"Geez, how do you keep track of all the lame rules in this place?"

"Riley, please!"

"OK, OK," Riley said. "I'll turn round and go back – I'll park by the boarding house and meet you there."

He gave her a wave as he drove off.

"So… are you two back on again?" Alice asked as soon as Riley was out of earshot.

"No," Georgie said. "But at least we're friends again."

Georgie had been the one to make the phone call in the end. She had phoned Riley to tell him how well

Princess had settled in and she also told him that it was over with James.

"Did you tell him why?" Alice asked.

Georgie shook her head. "I don't want to make Riley think that our break-up was his fault, because it wasn't."

Finally things were going well with Riley, and Georgie didn't want to put too much pressure on their relationship. It was a big step already that he'd agreed to come along to watch the polo with her. Considering he was virtually allergic to Blainford the fact that he was willing to be here for her must mean something.

It was a cold day and Riley was pulling on his lumberjack coat and beanie as the girls arrived back at their dorm.

"Are you ready to go?" he asked Georgie.

"We just need to change into our school whites," Georgie said. "It's a special event so they make us wear a different uniform for it."

Riley waited outside while the girls got changed into their white jerseys and skirts and their navy-blue woollen winter blazers.

As they walked up the school driveway the other

Blainford pupils were also dressed in their whites. Some of the students on the driveway were obviously riding later that day and were already in their polo breeches with brown knee-high polo boots and pads, and their house colours. Each of them wore a numbered shirt emblazoned with a giant number from one to four depending on their team position.

"How many teams are there?" Riley asked.

"About thirty," Alice said. "It's a big competition."

"So explain to me why you're not riding?"

"Georgie!" Alice was shocked. "You haven't told him yet? Oh, come on! You have to tell him about Conrad!"

Georgie glared at Alice, wishing she would shut up. She hadn't wanted to tell Riley because she was pretty certain that he would go after Conrad. Which would only make matters worse. Right now, she was pretty good at making things worse herself without getting Riley into trouble too.

"I got into a scrape on the field." Georgie tried to downplay it. "It was unfair, but the upshot is that the headmistress sort of banned us girls from the competition this year."

"It's not the headmistress's fault," Alice added. "The polo master totally has it in for Georgie. He doesn't think that girls should play polo."

There were four polo fields set up on the main grounds directly opposite the entrance to the school quad. Each polo field was almost twice the size of a football field and between the fields tiered grandstands had been erected for pupils to sit on. For the teachers and parents there were four white marquee tents where champagne and caviar were being served.

"Isn't there any real food?" Riley grumbled as he passed the caviar tents and took up his bench seat. "What good is a bunch of little black fish eggs? They should have hotdogs and fries!"

The students were quickly filling up the stands and they didn't have long to wait until the first games began. The first match on the main field was between a Luhmuhlen team and a team from Lexington House. It didn't get off to a very exciting start. The play was muddled and none of the players seemed to be capable of connecting with the ball accurately. The referee kept calling fouls as mallets swung wildly through the air and players miscued their hits and caught the ponies on their wraps. The ball volleyed pointlessly from one end of the field to the other without either team ever looking likely to score a goal. It was tedious to watch and by the end of the first chukka the score was nil-nil.

"Are you kidding me?" Alice shook her head in disbelief.

"We could have totally creamed these guys," Emily said. "They don't even know how to play."

"Seriously?" Riley said. "So you guys are better than this?"

"Way, way better!" Georgie said.

It was frustrating to watch the next three chukkas, but the girls persevered because the next Luhmuhlen team was Cameron, Alex, JP and Mark.

The boys had been originally rostered to play against a Lexington team, but because Badminton House had been cut, an entirely different polo side were taking the field against them.

"I don't believe it," Alice winced. "It's Conrad."

The players rode out and Georgie watched as Conrad

and James, both dressed in their ice-blue polo shirts, came up the centre of the field in a rising canter. James's eyes raked the stands and when he caught sight of Georgie and Riley together his face turned dark. Conrad, meanwhile, rode straight up to the sidelines, raising his mallet to Georgie.

"Hey, Parker," he shouted, "you wanna be my stick chick? Since you're not playing you might as well be holding my mallet!"

"You're a total numnah, Conrad!" Alice shouted back at him. "Leave her alone."

"What's going on?" Riley said. "Who is that guy?"

"That's Conrad," Alice said. "He's the one who pushed Georgie off her horse. He's the reason we're not playing."

"What?" Riley was furious. "He pushed you off your horse?"

"Uh-huh," Alice answered for her. "He's a jerk. He's been giving Georgie a hard time all term."

"It's no big deal," Georgie said. "Honestly, Riley."

"Have you told the school about this? It sounds like he's bullying you!"

"I've tried to tell the teachers," Georgie said, "but it only makes it worse."

"Georgie! He can't behave like that! You should have told me—"

"This is why I didn't tell you! I knew you'd react like this." Georgie shook her head. "Please, Riley, just leave it."

Riley sat in the stands, his arms folded, eyes narrowed as he watched Conrad galloping up and down, waving his mallet like a poseur.

"Ohmygod!" Daisy said. "Check out Kennedy's outfit!"

On the sidelines where the spare Burghley House horses were ready and waiting for the next chukka, Kennedy was standing with Arden and Tori. The showjumperettes were all dressed in their school whites, but somehow Kennedy had managed to get hers altered. Her jersey was now almost two sizes too small and hugged her curves. Her school skirt had at least ten centimetres cut off the hemline so that it grazed the top of her thigh. She had her hair slicked back in a ponytail and was wearing gold sunglasses as she stood holding a mallet in her hands.

"A born stick chick!" Alice groaned.

"What's a stick chick?" Riley asked.

"A girl who hangs out with the polo boys and thinks it's a big thrill to hold their mallet for them," Daisy said.

"So that Kennedy girl is Conrad's stick chick?" Riley asked.

"Uh-huh. She's Conrad's girlfriend."

The chukka got underway and right from the start the game was evenly matched. The girls were shouting themselves hoarse cheering for Alex, Cameron and JP. The referee was right in the thick of it, but all the same Conrad tried his usual tricks. Georgie saw him totally cut off Cam and try to shove him when the ref wasn't looking. James, meanwhile, seemed to be deliberately targeting JP.

"Foul!" Georgie shouted as James shoulder-slammed JP off the ball. The score so far was one-all to Burghley – this was going to be close!

Riley looked at his watch and stood up. "Hey, Georgie, I'll be back in a minute, OK?"

"Huh?" Georgie looked up at him. "OK, sure."

When the chukka came to a close the score was three-two to Luhmuhlen.

"Ohmygod!" Emily was bouncing up and down in her seat. "I can't believe Luhmuhlen have got the lead and—"

"Hey!" Alice looked over at the Burghley House team camp. "What is Riley doing? Why is he over there?"

Georgie looked over at the Burghley House riders who were now heading back to their camp to remount on fresh horses. She could see Kennedy, Arden and Tori and standing there talking to them was... Riley.

"Uh-oh," Alice said. "I've got a bad feeling about this."

"Ohmygod!" Georgie pushed past the girls, and ran down the steps of the grandstand and on to the polo field.

As she raced across the polo field she could see Riley talking to Kennedy. The head showjumperette was flirting madly with him, giggling and hair flicking for all she was worth. But Georgie knew that Riley wasn't really interested in Kennedy – he was just waiting for Conrad. Georgie could see him eyeing up the Burghley

House captain as he dismounted and led his pony over to join his girlfriend.

"Riley!" Georgie shouted.

Riley looked up at her and smiled. "Hey, Georgie. I'll be with you in a second, I've just got to have a quick word with Kennedy's boyfriend."

Smiling politely, Riley turned to Kennedy. "Can I have your mallet for a moment?"

He took the polo stick from her hands and walked straight up to the Burghley House head prefect. In one swift manoeuvre he shoved Conrad up against the wall of the polo shed, the mallet rammed into the cleft of his throat so that it was pressed up against his windpipe.

Choking and gasping, Conrad tried to push him away, but Riley was stronger than him and he held him pinned to the wall, while Kennedy and the showjumperettes watched in horror.

"You think you're tough, huh?" Riley said. "Hassling first-year girls and pushing them off their horses? That makes you a big man?"

"I... don't know what you're talking about..." Conrad managed to choke out the words.

"Oh, I think you do, Con-rad," Riley spat out the prefect's name in two syllables. "But here's the thing. You can't bully me. I don't go to this school. You can't give me Fatigues for walking on some sissy patch of grass. You have no jurisdiction over me."

"I didn't—" Conrad tried to speak, but Riley shushed him.

"I'm not here to argue with you, Conrad. I'm here to tell you that this ends now. If you so much as look at Georgie the wrong way again, I'll come after you and I'll take those shiny prefect's spurs that you're wearing and use them on you in ways you don't even want to think about. Now do you understand me?"

Conrad nodded and Riley suddenly released his grip on the Burghley House head prefect's throat. Conrad reeled back, wheezing and gasping. Riley handed the polo mallet back to a stunned Kennedy.

The other Burghley players had finally noticed the drama and James dismounted his horse and made a beeline for Riley.

"What are you doing here? I told you not to come to Blainford," James said.

"Don't push your luck, James." Riley shot him down. "I took it easy on Conrad – you might not be so lucky."

For a brief moment James looked like he might have the guts to square up to Riley, but he just glared at him and then stormed off.

"Come on, Georgie," Riley reached out to take her hand, "the next chukka is about to begin. Let's get back to our seats. I want to see Luhmuhlen whump these guys!"

Georgie was so shell-shocked she didn't say a word all the way back to the stands. She took her seat and watched with her friends as Conrad, white as a sheet, came back on the field for the second chukka. Luhmuhlen totally dominated the next three chukkas to win the game.

The other girls had been watching the whole drama from the stands. They said nothing to Riley about it, but after the game was over and they were back at the dorm they couldn't talk about anything else.

"It was just about the coolest thing I have ever seen," Alice gushed. "The look on Conrad's face! And there's Kennedy just watching with her mouth hanging open."

"I'm not a fan of violence," Emily said, "but Alice is right – that was way, way cool!"

The true impact of what had happened on the field that day didn't sink in until Georgie was leaving the boarding house for dinner and found the brown paper package sitting on the doorstep addressed to her. She opened the brown wrapper up and looked inside.

Conrad must have had a word with his girlfriend. Kennedy had returned her Barbour.

Chapter Thirteen

*I*n school assembly the following Monday morning the results from the Round Robin were announced. Four teams had played their way through to the semifinals, including JP, Alex and Cam's team.

Even though they'd been unable to play, the girls got a certain satisfaction from the sight of James and Conrad squirming in their seats as their Burghley House team was noted as being knocked out in the first round.

"The finals are being held on the school fields on Saturday," Mrs Dickins-Thomson continued. "Please advise your parents if they are planning to come along that this is a day earlier than the original scheduled date to avoid clashing with the Bluegrass Cup being held in

Frankfort on Sunday. I am sure that many of our budding polo stars will relish the opportunity to go along to watch the games in Frankfort so we've moved our finals to accommodate this. For those pupils who wish to attend the Bluegrass Cup, there will be a bus departing the school at nine am."

"Are we planning to go?" Emily asked as they left assembly on their way to Ms Schmidt's German class.

"I saw a poster for it in town," Georgie said. "It seems like it's a big deal."

"It's a big competition," Alice said. "I went last year with Kendal and Cherry. There're lots of games for all the different goal rankings. There's a qualifier on Saturday and then the finals on the Sunday."

"We should go and watch," Emily said. "We might pick up some pointers."

"Forget going to watch," Daisy said. "We should go and play."

The others stopped in their tracks.

"Are you serious?" Alice said.

"Why not?" Daisy said. "It's a competition for different goal rankings, right? We're all minus-two players so we'd be at the bottom of the league – it's not like we'd be up against the hardcore ten-goalers."

"Even if we're playing low grade," Emily said, "these aren't school games. These are grown-ups with proper teams and strings of expensive ponies paid for by wealthy patrons."

"It's still polo," Daisy said. "We know how to play and we've got the string. The ponies are ready for it."

"She's got a point," Alice agreed. "We could enter."

"Aren't we supposed to be at the finals of the Round Robin on Saturday though?" Emily said. "And that's when the Bluegrass Qualifier takes place."

"We could always wriggle out of the Round Robin somehow," Daisy said. "It's not like we're actually playing."

"I dunno," Emily said, "what do you think, Georgie?"

"Come on, Georgie," Daisy said. "Are we in?"

Georgie didn't know what to say. When Mrs Dickins-Thomson had turfed the girls' team out of the Round Robin it had been such a miserable anticlimax after all their hard work. She had tried not to let it get to her, but she'd taken it hard. Now they had a chance to prove themselves, not just against their Blainford rivals, but against real polo players. It was too good to be true.

"We're in," Georgie said. "Let's go play ourselves some polo."

✳

Before dawn on Saturday morning, when the boarders and the teachers were all still sleeping, two horse trucks entered the gates of the Blainford Academy and drove along the driveway, turning left to pull up outside the Burghley House stables.

Georgie was standing waiting in the darkness for their arrival. She directed the first truck down the side of the stables and then directed the second truck to park right beside it.

Riley jumped out of the cab. "Are you ready to go?" he called out to her.

"Shhh!" Georgie put a finger to her lips. "We're trying not to wake anyone, remember?"

"Where are the horses?" Riley whispered.

"The girls are just putting their trucking boots on," Georgie said. "And then we can get out of here. Could you help me to carry some saddles?"

"Sure."

As they headed into the stables to get the tack, the door of the second truck cab swung open and a skinny, hunched man wearing a trucker's cap leapt out.

"Need some help with your gear, ma'am?"

"Thanks, Kenny," Georgie smiled at him.

"No problem," Kenny said. Or at least that was what Georgie thought he said. Kenny always had his mouth so full of chewing tobacco that it was impossible to understand a word he was saying. He was Riley's uncle and he worked right here at Blainford as the school's caretaker.

"The thing is, Kenny," Georgie began to explain, "we're not really supposed to be going off school grounds. I don't want you to get into trouble by helping us."

The girls had considered their options when it came to entering the Bluegrass Cup Qualifier. They could confess all to Mrs Dickins-Thomson and ask for official school permission to attend, but none of them fancied their chances. Far better to bunk off during the Round Robin and go rogue.

"No one will notice if we're not there," Alice reasoned. "Kendal and the others will cover for us at breakfast if anyone asks where we are."

"We need to be out of here before dawn so no one sees us leaving," Georgie said.

Alice agreed. "It'd be pretty hard explaining where you were going with sixteen horses!"

Riley offered to help them straight away – but with sixteen horses to transport it would take two trucks. And that was where Kenny came in.

"I don't want to get you into trouble, Kenny," Georgie said as he lowered the truck ramp. "If we get caught, you might lose your job or something."

Kenny chewed thoughtfully on his tobacco. "The wife would love that," he said. "Then I'd have the time to build that chicken coop she's been nagging me about."

He grinned at Georgie and she saw the brown bits of chewing tobacco stuck to his teeth. "Now, which horses are we putting on this one, and where are we headin'?"

Georgie smiled. "Take us to the Bluegrass Cup!"

✳

As they drove through the gates of the academy, it suddenly struck Georgie that they were wilfully disobeying Blainford rules by leaving the school. More than that, they were taking sixteen horses with them! This was not a casual disobedience, like walking on the quad. If they were caught, she didn't even want to think about the trouble they would be in. She felt match-day nerves grip her, twisting a knot in her tummy.

As they rolled in at 6am the polo grounds were already busy. Many of the teams had arrived the day before, and slept in their trucks overnight. Their ponies were kept penned in the yards beside them and the grooms were hard at work mucking out, feeding and watering. Georgie watched one groom working three ponies at once, mounted up on one and leading two others alongside her. The ponies were all immaculate, well-muscled with tails professionally taped and tack polished to perfection. The groom wore a shirt emblazoned with her patron's logo. Many of these teams playing today had corporate sponsors who had spent hundreds of thousands of dollars to buy the best ponies and players. The sponsors had their own marquees along the sidelines of the four polo fields where the action would take place.

As Riley eased the truck past the wash bays and parked in a vacant space, Georgie reached down beneath the seat of the truck and pulled out a piece of paper.

"Is that the schedule? What time do we play?" Daisy asked.

"Our game is at nine."

Kenny parked his truck alongside Riley and the riders all jumped out and dropped the ramps ready to unload.

"I'll go to the office and check on our registration," Alice offered. She strode off across the field.

"Let's get started," Georgie said. "We've got sixteen horses to bandage and tails to put up."

"We're taping tails, remember," Daisy instructed

241

Georgie and Emily. "No Argie knots today – this is competition standard."

The girls busied themselves doing the legs, taking off the trucking boots and replacing them with polo wraps while Riley and Kenny unloaded all the tack from the trucks.

"We so badly need grooms!" Daisy looked over enviously at the trucks where the polo players were lounging about and chatting over their coffee.

"This is a crew ship, Daisy, not a luxury liner," Georgie sighed.

"It's not a luxury – we need them," Daisy pointed out. "Who's going to keep the ponies warm, hang on to our sticks and run the pony lines for us between chukkas?"

"Me and Kenny will cope," Riley said. "We know the drill."

"We'll saddle our first two ponies up to save time," Georgie explained to Daisy and Emily. "When we come off after the first chukka, Riley and Kenny will take the saddles off our ponies and swap them on to the ones we're riding in the third chukka. Then they'll ride up the pony lines to warm up and have them standing by ready for us as we come off the field.

"Which field are you on?" Riley asked.

"I don't know yet," Georgie said.

"Here comes Alice," Emily said. "Let's see what she's found out."

"Ohmygod!" Alice had arrived back from the registration tent and she looked totally psyched.

"I was just at the registration table signing us up and Adolfo Cambiaso was queuing right behind me! He is, like, a polo god! A ten-goal player. And he spoke to me!"

"What did he say?" Emily looked amazed.

"He said, 'Are you in the right queue? This one is for the players.' I told him I was a player, but I don't think he believed me."

Emily looked nervous. "We're not playing against him are we? Because that would be, like, insane."

Alice shook her head. "We're in the low grade league, up against the Versailles Cavaliers. They're a varsity team."

"What's varsity?" Emily asked.

"Like university, only American," Daisy explained.

"Does that mean they're older than us?"

"Look around, Emily," Alice said. "The grass here is older than us."

"So what field are we on?" Georgie asked Alice.

"Number three – the one over there underneath the trees. The game starts at eight-thirty."

"Eight-thirty?" Georgie squeaked. "I thought it was nine."

Alice shrugged. "Not on the schedule in the tent it isn't."

"What's the time now?" Georgie asked.

"Seven-fifteen," Riley replied.

"Less talk and more bandaging!" Georgie said. "We need all of these ponies ready in one hour."

By eight-fifteen the girls had their ponies saddled and ready on the sidelines of field number three, that was where they got their first glimpse of the Cavaliers.

"You're kidding me!" Emily said. "We're up against them?"

The Cavaliers were fully grown men with broad

shoulders and legs that were so long they could have powered the ponies along with their feet.

"Well what did you expect?" Daisy said matter-of-factly. "This is an open league game."

Emily groaned. "They're going to cream us."

"They are if you think negatively like that," Alice snapped at her. "I didn't smuggle sixteen horses out of Blainford Academy so that I could go down in the first round!"

"Our size is our advantage," Georgie insisted. "These guys won't rate us as competition. They certainly won't consider us to be a threat. But we're small and we're fast. If we play an attacking game right from the start, before they know what's hit them we can get some points on the board."

"Uh, question?" Daisy raised her hand. "We're all talking tactics, but someone actually has to run the show once we're on the field, right?"

"You mean a captain?" Alice asked.

Daisy nodded. "I think it should be Georgie. She knows the rule book back to front."

"But Alice is the better player," Georgie said.

"No," Alice shook her head. "You should be our captain, Georgie. You're better at making the calls and besides, you started all of this."

"Totally," Emily agreed, doing a mock salute. "Ready for your orders, captain."

✳

As the girls took to the field they looked absurdly out of place lining up against men who were twice their size. The Cavaliers captain in the number one jersey took one look at his competition and raised his mallet to appeal to the referee.

"Hey, ref! Who rostered us on to play a bunch of girls?" he demanded. "Call the organisers over to sort this out!"

Georgie cantered up to the Cavaliers captain. "There's nothing to sort out. You're supposed to be playing us."

"I'm not playing with girls."

"What are you, five years old? Of course you're playing us. Unless you want to forfeit the game."

"Yeah," Alice shouted out, backing her up. "We're here to play, so let's play."

The Cavaliers captain turned to the referee. "This is a joke!"

"Well, I'm not laughing and neither are they," the referee responded. "Come on, you're holding up play. Let's get this game started."

As the bell sounded the Badminton girls leaped straight into action, Georgie winning the throw-in and sending a shot blasting through the players towards Daisy in centre field. Before the Cavaliers could even mount an attack, Alice was up at Daisy's side to receive the pass. There were two Cavaliers close on her tail, but she stayed focused and cantered up on Desiray to take a shot at the goal with a powerful forehand swing. The ball shot straight between the posts. Badminton had their first points on the board after less than a minute of play!

Shocked by this sudden goal the Cavaliers tried to regroup, but they had no idea how to deal with this pack of young players. The girls were small and swift and made the men look like they were laden with sandbags.

Alice, Emily and Daisy had chosen Dupree ponies for the first chukka, but Georgie had decided to ride Belle as the mare was quick on the break and utterly fearless.

When Georgie took the ball off a Cavalier and made a sprint up the field towards her goal, Belle proved her worth by out-galloping two Cavaliers and then shoulder-barging another so that Georgie could take her shot. The first Cavalier she'd passed was trying to ride up the other side to block the goal mouth, but Daisy rode him off with a knee-barge to leave the goal open so that Georgie could shoot and score. Goal number two!

The score was two-nil to the girls as they came off the field.

In the pony lines Riley was already standing by with Georgie's next mare, Jet. Georgie dismounted and mounted up again, but she noticed that the Cavaliers had a far cooler way of swapping horses. They simply got their grooms to line their new mounts up alongside them and then vaulted from one horse to the next so that their feet never touched the ground.

"You see?" Daisy said, watching the Cavaliers. "This is why we need our own grooms!"

"Well, it's not helping them win the game, is it?" Alice pointed out as she dismounted and grabbed Will's reins from Kenny.

"They'll take us seriously from now on," Georgie pointed out. "They're going to come back at us with everything they've got in the second chukka."

"Well then, we need to raise our game," Alice said.

Georgie turned to Emily. "You're doing a great job in defence. This time do some big shots up the field and Alice and I will chase the ball where it lands."

"What about me?" Daisy asked.

"You're our Hell-raiser," Georgie said. "Drop back from your frontline position and tackle hard every time they get the ball, ride them off their line."

"But they'll get a penalty if I foul them!"

"The ref's not going to call foul on you!" Alice said. "You're just a girl, remember? How can a girl foul some big guy on a varsity team?"

In the second chukka Daisy rode so hard at the Cavalier's players that at one point she almost knocked the number three off his horse.

"It wasn't on purpose!" Daisy objected. "I was just trying to get the ball."

By the end of chukka two the Cavaliers had managed one goal to the girls' two. The score was now four-one to the Badminton House team and on the sidelines a crowd was beginning to gather.

By chukka three the Cavaliers came back with a vengeance, but the girls were ready for them.

"We're already in the lead so the next two chukkas should be all about defence," Georgie said. "I'm going to stay back with Emily to protect the goal; Alice and Daisy, you're on your own."

It was a sound tactic. The Cavaliers simply couldn't get the ball past Georgie and Emily and when they made a crucial mistake in a lineout Alice capitalised on it, sent a pass up to Daisy and the three girls watched as Daisy went on alone against two Cavaliers, rode them off and made the goal!

There were cheers from the sideline as the girls took to the field for the final chukka ahead by five points to one. The Cavaliers had a no-prisoners attitude, but they got called for fouling when one of them got too rough with Emily and there was a penalty shot from the goal mouth. Daisy shot the ball screaming through the goal. The girls had won in a landslide – six points to one!

There was a huge roar from the crowd as the final

bell went. On the field the girls hugged before pulling themselves together and organising their horses in a line to ride up and shake hands with the Versailles Cavaliers.

"Good game," Georgie smiled at the Cavaliers captain as he shook her hand. "Whatever," he grunted in reply.

"They weren't very good sports about it, were they?" Emily said as the girls left the field.

"Think about it from their point of view," Alice said. "It must be like losing to your kid sister."

"Shameful," Daisy agreed.

The girls were heading back towards the sidelines when a man with a thick thatch of jet-black hair came out of the crowd and strode across the field towards them.

"Congratulations, Georgie," he called out. "An unexpected win – I imagine it will be the upset of the day."

The man looked smug as he added, "Especially since you aren't meant to be here."

Georgie was mortified. She was face to face with the last person she had expected or wanted to see. It was Heath Brompton, the Blainford Academy polo master.

Chapter Fourteen

*T*he thrill of victory was short-lived.

"I have no idea how you girls organised this little escapade," Heath Brompton said, "and I'm not about to discuss it now. Clearly you have contravened Blainford rules and you are out of school bounds without permission."

"But, sir—" Georgie started. But Mr Brompton cut her dead.

"We are not discussing this, Parker. Get your horses loaded on the trucks and get them back to school. You will meet me at Mrs Dickins-Thomson's office this afternoon at four and we'll resolve this matter then."

It was a grim ride back in the horse truck. Nobody spoke. Back at the stables they unloaded the polo ponies and led them back to their boxes, rugging them up and leaving them with their hard feeds. By the time they were done it was only twelve o'clock. They had another four hours to kill before they were due at the headmistress's office.

"We could go and watch the end of the Round Robin," Emily suggested.

"What's the point?" Alice said. "We're already in trouble; I don't think turning up for the second half of the tournament is going to dig us out of this mess."

"I didn't mean that," Emily said. "It's just that Alex is playing and I thought it would take our minds off things, you know, until the meeting."

"What do you think Mrs Dickins-Thomson is going to do to us?" Daisy asked. "Do you think we could be expelled?"

"Ohmygod!" Emily was shocked. "Mum and Dad are going to kill me!"

"Whoa!" Alice raised her hands. "Everybody calm down. You're blowing this out of proportion!"

"No, I'm not," Daisy said. "We were off school property without permission. That's suspension at least!"

Emily groaned. "I wish the meeting was now. I want to get it over and done with."

"Come on," Georgie said. "Let's go and change into our whites and watch the polo until we're called to the gallows."

✳

The Luhmuhlen game helped to relieve the tension as the girls cheered for Cam, Alex and JP. It was a good game too – the boys narrowly losing to a very good Lexington team in the semifinal round. As the clock ticked closer to 4pm, Georgie tried to focus on watching the final match, but all she could think about was the trouble they were in – and the fact that it was all her fault.

"No, it's not," Daisy insisted as the four girls walked up the driveway after the last game, heading for Mrs Dickins-Thomson's office. "It was my idea that we go and play the Bluegrass Qualifier."

"You mustn't blame yourself, Georgie," Emily added. "We knew the risks. We wanted to play badly enough to take them."

Georgie shook her head. "There's no reason for us all to get expelled. Let me tell Mrs Dickins-Thomson that it was my idea and I made you guys do it."

"You're not really grasping the whole team spirit thing, are you?" Alice replied. "We're in this together. That's how this started and that's how it will end, OK?"

"Yeah, Georgie," Daisy agreed. "There is no 'I' in team."

"There's a 'me' though, if you jumble it up," Emily added.

The others stared at her.

"It's just a joke," Emily said. "You know, to lighten the mood before we all get expelled."

At the top of the stairs Heath Brompton was waiting for them at the door of Mrs Dickins-Thomson's office. Georgie could have sworn she saw a satisfied smirk pass over the face of the polo master as he ushered them in.

Four chairs were already lined up waiting for them in front of Mrs Dickins-Thomson's desk and the headmistress was standing there, beckoning for them to take a seat.

"Mr Brompton has filled me in on the rather surprising developments at the Bluegrass Cup," Mrs Dickins-Thomson said. "I cannot believe you girls would defy school rules and take yourselves off to a polo competition without permission. Do you understand the distress and embarrassment you might have caused if something had happened to you? No one from the school even knew where you were!"

"Yes, they did—" Emily began her sentence and Georgie panicked. Emily was going to blab that Kenny had been there with them. If Mrs Dickins-Thomson found out, the school caretaker could be fired! Thinking fast, Georgie lashed out and gave Emily a brutal kick under the desk.

"Ow!"

Mrs Dickins-Thomson frowned. "I'm sorry?"

"Yes, ma'am," Georgie said hastily. "You're right. No one at the school knew where we were – but there were four of us there, and we're old enough to look after ourselves."

"Four of you – and sixteen horses!" Mrs Dickins-Thomson pointed out. "You are responsible for the care of these animals. Taking them off school property and going to an open event like this is unthinkable. And Mr Brompton told me you were up against the Versailles Cavaliers! You could easily have been hurt playing against grown men!"

"Not the way they played!" Alice couldn't help muttering.

"I'm sorry? What do you mean, Alice?" Mrs Dickins-Thomson said.

"I mean those guys never laid a hand on us," Alice said. "They weren't fast enough. And they weren't very good sports about it either."

Mrs Dickins-Thomson stared at Alice. "Alice Dupree. Are you telling me that your team won? That you actually beat the Versailles Cavaliers?"

"Totally!" Alice said. "We whupped them by six goals to one."

Mrs Dickins-Thomson was stunned. "But they're a top varsity team, aren't they?"

"Uh-huh," Alice said.

"Did Mr Brompton not tell you that we won?" Georgie asked. "He was there when we came off the field."

Mr Brompton, who had been standing by the door all this time with his arms folded, suddenly looked rather uncomfortable.

"Mr Brompton?" Mrs Dickins-Thomson turned to him. "Is this true? Did the girls actually win the qualifier?"

Heath Brompton coughed awkwardly. "Did I not mention that bit?" he asked.

"No," Mrs Dickins-Thomson replied stiffly. "You did not."

She turned back to the girls. "So if you won your qualifier I take it you've progressed to the next round tomorrow?"

Georgie nodded. "We're scheduled to play in the low goal category, obviously, because we're all minus-two players."

Mrs Dickins-Thomson stood up from her chair. She looked suddenly animated, almost excited.

"Mr Brompton," she turned to her polo master. "Please go down to the stables and prepare two of the school horse trucks for the morning. And we'll need polo jerseys. And can you send Mrs Dubois in to see me?"

"I'm sorry?" Heath Brompton looked confused. "Polo jerseys?"

"Yes, in the school colours obviously. The boys' jerseys in the small size should fit the girls."

"What's all this for?"

"The Bluegrass Cup, Mr Brompton!" Mrs Dickins-Thomson said. "The girls are playing for Blainford Academy. They must be wearing the school colours."

The headmistress turned back to Georgie. "When Mrs Dubois arrives we'll organise anything else you need. She can sort out your entry details. It's a bit last-minute, but we'll make an announcement at the dining hall tonight that there will be a second bus provided to the venue so that any students who wish to come along tomorrow in view of this news can also attend."

"So you're letting us play?" Georgie couldn't believe it. "You're not going to expel us?"

"Miss Parker, why on earth would I do that?" Mrs Dickins-Thomson looked shocked at the notion. "Blainford is in the finals for the Bluegrass Cup. You and your team have the opportunity to bring great honour upon the academy. This is marvellous news!"

As she shut the door behind them the girls all breathed a sigh of relief.

"Wow," Emily said.

"We're playing for the glory of Blainford Academy," Daisy added.

"So why is it," Georgie asked, "that I feel even more terrified now than I did when I came in here?"

✳

The next morning at 5am, the girls loaded their ponies up in the trucks once more.

Georgie had clambered up into the cab alongside Emily with Kenny at the wheel and they were just about to set off when there was a tap at the passenger window. Georgie got the shock of her life when she peered out into the darkness and saw Tara Kelly standing outside.

"I wanted to wish you good luck before you set off," Tara said.

"Thanks," Georgie said.

"I'll be escorting the pupils on the nine o'clock bus, so I'll be in the stands watching you," Tara said.

Georgie was about to wind her window back up again when Tara spoke again.

"Georgie, that grey mare, the dapple one?"

"Yeah?"

"She's your best horse. If I were you I'd save her for the last chukka."

As they drove down the Versailles highway towards Frankfort, Georgie tried to think about her tactics for the match. It wasn't easy focusing, however, with Emily burbling on in the seat alongside her.

"I can't help it. I talk when I'm nervous," Emily said.

"Having a few nerves is good," Georgie assured her. "It gets the adrenalin moving."

"What about if you have so many nerves that you think you might throw up?"

"You feel sick?" Kenny glanced at her. "Chewin' tobacco is the best thing to settle a stomach," Kenny said. "It's got medicinal properties."

Emily watched with revulsion as Kenny took another wad from his pouch of tobacco on the dashboard and shoved it into his mouth, exposing his tobacco-stained teeth in the process.

"I am definitely going to be sick," Emily groaned.

The two trucks marked with the Blainford Academy emblem rolled in convoy through the gates of the Frankfort polo grounds.

Kenny turned past the fields and headed for the same parking bay they had occupied the day before.

He pulled the truck to a stop and Georgie jumped out and lowered her ramp. Beside her, Heath Brompton parked the second truck. Georgie gave him a smile, but the polo master didn't smile back. He looked his usual surly self as he dropped the ramp and went inside the truck to get the horses.

"I don't think he's very happy working for a bunch of girls," Emily said as she stood watching the polo master who was leading out Jocasta and Jet.

"Some of us, on the other hand, don't have a problem with it."

It was Cameron Fraser. He was dressed in his polo whites and standing there with Alex, JP and Riley.

"Your stick chicks," Cam said, taking a bow, "reporting for duty."

"I didn't know boys could actually be 'stick chicks'," Georgie said.

"Well, you can call us mallet men if you like," Cameron said. "We're here to do your bidding. We'll groom your horses, prepare them for battle and warm them up between chukkas."

"Plus," Alex added, smiling at Emily, "we'll stand on the sidelines and scream and cheer for you and we'll be waiting here to kiss you if you win."

"Cool," Emily said. "I always wanted my own personal groupie."

"I think we're a bit better than groupies!" Riley said. "We're an integral part of the team!"

"Of course," Georgie agreed with a smile. "Now go and get my ponies ready for me, will you?"

"Yes, ma'am!"

As the boys bandaged the ponies, Georgie, Alice, Daisy and Emily put on their whites, their pads and their jerseys. Today, instead of the Badminton House colours, they wore the Blainford Academy school colours. Dark navy polo shirts with a pale blue sash stripe across the front and a silver crest on their breast pockets.

"I think I'd rather be saddling up than just standing here getting nervous," Alice said as she put on her boots.

Georgie looked at her watch. It was ten o'clock and they were due on the playing field in half an hour. "Let's make good use of the time we've got," she told the others, "and go and check out the competition."

The draw for the Bluegrass Cup had been posted that morning. The girls were up for the low-grade title game against the Winchester Reserves.

"Do we have any inside information on them?" Emily asked.

"Alice has been doing some digging," Georgie said. "Alice?"

"The Winchester is a very established polo club," Alice said. "They've been around for over a hundred years. They're pretty fancy too – posh grounds and all that. These guys are their low goal team, but they're pretty handy. And they're not exactly known for being clean players – they've got a rep for unnecessary fouling and rough play."

"What are their team colours?" Daisy asked.

"Yellow and black, " Alice said. "Keep an eye out for them."

"Uhhh, guys?" Emily said quietly. "I think I might have just found them."

She pointed over to the far side of the warm-up field where four men, dressed in bright yellow jerseys ringed with thick black bands, were warming up.

"Those guys are huge!" Daisy said.

"They're not men – they're mountains," Emily said.

The girls watched as the Winchester number one lined up against number three and then intentionally rammed him so that their horses bashed up against each other in a bone-crunching display of aggression.

"Whoa! If they treat their own horses like that, what's it going to be like to play against them?" Daisy said.

"Ohmygod!" Emily whimpered. "Does anyone else here suddenly miss the Cavaliers?"

"We can still outrun them," Daisy said. "Play it like we did last time?"

Georgie shook her head. "It won't work. They'll have seen the way we played against the Cavaliers and they'll be expecting it. If we try to run they'll ride us down."

"Well, then what are we going to do, Georgie?" Emily said. "They're gonna crush us."

"No," Georgie said. "They're not… because we're gonna crush them first."

Chapter Fifteen

*T*he buses from Blainford Academy arrived at the polo grounds at nine and the students in their whites and navy blazers cut a swathe through the crowd. Mrs Dickins-Thomson and Tara Kelly led the way to the grandstands.

"No chewing gum, Mr Blackburn," the headmistress instructed as one of the boys walked past. "Take your hands out of your pockets, Mr Adams, and stop slouching! You are representing your school so stand up straight, please."

As the students took their seats, filling five rows of the grandstand, Heath Brompton emerged from the riders' area. He looked around the crowded stands for somewhere to sit and then reluctantly took the seat next to Tara.

"Hello, Heath," Tara said. "How's the team looking?"

"Woefully underprepared," Heath replied. "They're going to disgrace the school. They aren't ready to play at this level."

Tara frowned. "I've been watching the girls train and I'd have to disagree."

"Oh, so you're a polo expert now?" Heath shot back at her.

Tara shook her head in disbelief. "You've always been like this, Heath, even when we were at school together. Why is it so hard for you to grasp that the girls at Blainford are every bit as capable in every branch of equestrianism as the boys?"

Heath Brompton wasn't having it. "Girls shouldn't be playing polo. They shouldn't even be at the school," he muttered darkly. "If I had my way Blainford would still be a boys' school like it was back in nineteen-thirty-six."

Tara looked coolly at him. "Your attitude towards girls doesn't have anything to do with the fact that I whipped you completely in the end of the year rankings in cross-country in our senior year, does it? Or the fact that Miss Parker's mother, Ginny, was chosen to captain the school polo team over you?"

"Ginny Parker should never have been made captain," Heath Brompton snapped. "It should have been me!"

"Oh, dear!" Tara looked at him with mock surprise. "Have I hit a nerve?"

"You haven't changed at all," Heath snarled at her. "You're the same competitive shrew that you were when I was at school with you."

"And you are still the same small-minded sexist," Tara said sharply. "If I hear any more reports about you making it hard for girls in your polo class then I'll be taking it up with Mrs Dickins-Thomson. I'm sure she'd be very interested to hear about your antiquated views."

"You can't—"

Tara turned to him with her finger placed over her lips. "Sshhh, please, Mr Brompton. It looks like they are about to get underway and I do want to watch the game without interruption."

✳

Out on the practice field, Georgie watched the Blainford pupils taking their seats in the stands. "It looks like half the school has turned out to watch us," she said.

"Well, that settles it," Alice said, "we better not lose."

The girls were ready to make their entrance on to the field, mounted up on their first chukka ponies. They had chosen reliable, experienced mounts for the first quarter, each of them riding one of the polo mares that Mr Dupree had donated to the team. Daisy had chosen Jada, one of the Duprees' most experienced mares. Alice was on the veteran dun, Desiray. Emily was riding Vita, the pretty dark brown mare with four white socks.

Georgie was riding Estrella, the little chestnut with the white star on her forehead. Or at least she was planning to ride Estrella if the mare would stay still long enough to let her mount up. Estrella was so over-excited she refused to stand still, crab-stepping from side to side as Georgie bounced about beside her with one foot in the stirrup trying to get onboard.

"Here!" Riley stepped in to help her, hanging on to the mare until she could climb onboard. "Don't move, I need to tighten your girth."

Estrella stood still for a moment and then she raised

her head high and let out a clarion call, whinnying a challenge to the Winchester horses.

"She knows this is the real thing," Georgie said. "She's ready."

Riley looked anxiously over at the Winchester players. "Promise me you'll be careful out there?"

"You know me," Georgie said.

"Yeah," Riley replied. "I do. That's what worries me."

Alex was doing a final check on Emily's girth. He whispered last-minute advice to Emily, holding on to her hand, reluctant to let her go.

Cameron meanwhile, was busily checking Alice's martingale.

"Isn't there anything you want to tell me?" Alice said to him.

"Like what?"

Alice sighed. "I don't know, something poignant before I go on the field to face a team full of man-sized thugs who might kill me?"

Cameron snorted, trying to suppress a laugh. "Come off it, Alice! They're the ones that are in trouble here – I should be over there reading them their last rites."

Daisy rode over to join them. "Those guys have no idea what's coming at them."

Georgie turned Estrella round and addressed her team mates. "Does everyone understand the tactics for the game? Are we ready to do this?"

"We're ready," Alice affirmed.

"Sure," Emily said nervously.

"I think it's the craziest plan I've ever heard," Daisy said, "but, yeah. Let's do it."

"Remember," Georgie said, "we're going to come out in the first chukka and play a hard, fast and physical game. If they think they can ride us off our line just because they're bigger than us, they need to think again."

"If they come at you, never give away ground," Alice added. "Knee-barge them straight back."

"There's no way I'm letting them ride me off the ball," Daisy said. "They can forget about it."

Emily wasn't so sure. "I don't think I can ride off a guy twice my size."

"You don't have to get into the maul, Emily," Georgie reassured her. "Your job is defence. We're relying on you to stop the ball before it reaches the goal. You mustn't let them past."

Emily's face looked grim with determination. "Let's go."

✳

Out on the field, the four girls took up their positions in the lineout, squaring up to their opposite players. Georgie's eyes scanned the line for their number three player, a thick-set man with a moustache and russet brown hair. He was the captain and their best player and he would be their key goal scorer. She glanced over at Alice, who returned her look with a nod, confirming that she knew that this guy was the one that she had to watch.

At the far end of the lineout, Emily was keeping a tight hold on Vita, her game face set.

Georgie's last glance was to Daisy. She was right at the front of the lineout, wheeling Jada about, jostling for position against the Winchester number one as they waited for the ref to throw the ball in. Georgie turned Estrella on her hocks and focused, her muscles tensed and ready for the throw-in. This was it. Game on.

The bell rang and the ball flew across the grass towards the horses. Georgie reacted immediately on instinct, driving Estrella forward fearlessly, her polo stick clashing up against the Winchester number two as they fought for possession.

The ball shot out of the pack and whizzed across the field, heading in the direction of the Blainford goal. Daisy pressed Jada into a gallop and set off after it, but there were two Winchester riders following close behind her.

"Daisy!" Georgie called out. "You've got company!"

Daisy got to the ball first and hit it hard towards the goal posts. She tried to chase it up, but the Winchester number one was all over her, riding her off the line, barging against her with his knee and stealing the ball, taking it back in the other direction.

Daisy, however, wasn't deterred. Urging Jada into a gallop, she stayed with the Winchester rider, and then when the two mares were shoulder-to-shoulder, she pulled across, barged hard into the Winchester number one and swung a magnificent backhander so that the ball changed direction once more and shot back towards their goal.

"Alice!" Daisy cried out. "It's yours!"

As soon as Desiray caught sight of the white ball coming her way, the mare flattened back her ears and whipped her tail aggressively, giving chase at a gallop. There were two Winchester riders after the ball, but their mares weren't as fast as Desiray. There was no way she was letting anyone else get there before her. Alice tapped the ball towards the posts and Desiray swung her rump round to block the Winchester rider's path while her rider lined up a shot on goal. The mallet contacted the ball on the sweet spot and it flew cleanly between the posts.

In the stands the Blainford Academy students applauded. First blood to the Blainford girls!

The Winchester riders looked like stunned mullets as they came back to the line to restart the game. "Go after their number three!" the Winchester captain called to his men. "Somebody mark her!"

As the ref threw in, Alice tried to trap the ball with her mallet and send it to Georgie, but she was cut off by the Winchester number two who rode directly in front of her, barging into Desiray and swinging wildly with his stick right in front of the mare's legs.

"Foul! Ref, that was a total foul!" Daisy raised her mallet in the air to appeal to the referee, but the whistle wasn't blown. The game was still on and the number two player was off at a gallop and bearing down on Emily.

"Em!" Alice shouted out. "It's up to you!"

At the sight of the massive Winchester player thundering down on her Emily froze like a rabbit in headlights. And then, with a growl that sounded like a battle cry, she rode straight at him. Afterwards, Alice would say that it was like watching a jousting scene from a Robin Hood movie. Emily pushed Vita into a gallop and rode headlong at the Winchester number two, her mallet raised like a lance. The Winchester rider held his line. Emily was holding hers too – it was a game of chicken. Which one of them would scare first?

They were just a few strides apart when the Winchester player finally realised that this girl wasn't going to swerve out of his way. In a last-ditch bid to save himself he pulled the reins hard to the left. He managed to get his pony out of the way as Emily screamed down on the ball and hit it perfectly straight back up the field, where Alice, Georgie and Daisy were waiting to receive it and shoot once more for goal.

This time Daisy took the shot and it was a lucky hit. The ball glanced off the posts but went through. Goal number two to the Blainford girls!

As the girls came off after their first chukka they were ahead two points to nil and their ponies were exhausted and dripping with sweat.

"You're doing great out there," Riley told Georgie as he took hold of Estrella's reins while she vaulted down.

Georgie shook her head. "I'm not sure that we can hold them like this for the whole game. They're so much more physically strong than us."

"But you're better players," JP pointed out. "You can out-manoeuvre them."

"Do you think so?" Alice asked as she dismounted, utterly exhausted, from Desiray.

"I know so," Cameron confirmed. "Just keep passing, keep possession and keep taking shots at the goal. You can do this!"

The girls were on green Thoroughbreds for the second chukka. But what the ponies lacked in finesse they made up for with speed. This chukka was ridden so fast and furious, the ponies never seemed to stop galloping. The girls maintained their focus, trying to retain possession and fighting to keep the ball, but the Winchester players were getting more pushy. The Blainford girls seemed to spend half their time with their sticks in the air calling fouls, but the referee seemed blind to the Winchesters' dirty tactics. Winchester scored two goals in the first two minutes of the chukka. Then Blainford got one goal, a penalty from a foul. In the last minute of the chukka the Winchester number four made a blistering run down the wing and even Emily couldn't stop him. It was goal number three for the Winchester Reserves and the score was tied.

Riley was fuming as the girls left the field. "Somebody needs to have a talk with that referee! Those guys are fouling you constantly!"

"There's nothing we can do about it," Georgie said. "We've just got to keep in their faces."

The third chukka was the time to bring out their solid, dependable ponies. Georgie was mounted on Belle. Alice had Will and Emily was on Barclay. Daisy was on

Francine, who was already in a lather of anticipation before they even got on to the field.

From the start of the third chukka the Winchester riders had the lion's share of possession. Alice managed to snatch the ball away a couple of times and had two tries at goal, but each time the Winchester riders got in her way and she failed to score. Daisy finally got one through, managing to lay her mallet to the ball in the middle of a scrum of players and tapping it almost casually through the posts.

The hero of the third chukka though was definitely Emily. She blocked at least half a dozen attempts on goal by the Winchesters, sending the ball back up the line each time with her powerful field drives. In the end, despite their dominance, only two of the Winchester attempts on goal got through. It was enough for them to take the lead though and the score was now five-four against the girls.

Off the field on the pony lines the boys were ready and waiting as the girls came off the field to swap ponies for the final chukka. Riley had Princess all tacked up and Georgie rode Belle alongside so that the two mares were standing parallel. She dropped her feet loose of the stirrups and flung herself from Belle's back on to Princess.

Riley held the mares steady as she did this and then passed Georgie her mallet. "Be careful out there," he warned her. "These guys aren't going to hold back in the final chukka. They're going to foul you every chance they get."

"We're one point behind and there're only seven more minutes to go," Georgie said, taking up the reins. "How bad can it get?"

As it turned out, things got very bad indeed. In the first minute, Alice rode Nala hard into a lineout to take on a Winchester player and emerged with the mare holding up one of her forelegs.

"She's gone lame!" Alice was distraught as JP rushed on to the field to take Nala's reins. "I think one of the Winchester players must have clipped her with his mallet."

This was competition polo and the game didn't stop just because a pony was injured. The play continued up the field while Alice stood by impotently beside her injured mare.

"Leave Nala with me," JP instructed her. "You go get another horse."

On the sidelines, Cam and Alex were frantically saddling up Desiray.

"But she's already played!" Alice protested. "I need a fresh horse!"

"We don't have any back-up ponies," Cam said, fastening the surcingle at lightning speed and checking the girth before legging Alice back onboard. "Desiray played the first chukka. She's had enough time to recover."

Desiray seemed thrilled with the sudden turn of events. The dun mare was glad to be given a second chance on the field. But the time on the clock had been ticking by. As Alice re-entered the fray, the game was now well into the second half of the final chukka and still the girls hadn't managed to put vital points on the board.

Over the next few minutes there were cries of anguish from the Blainford fans as Daisy had a good line to the posts not once but twice, and each time her shots were thwarted by Winchester riders. There was a hard thwack at one point when the polo ball bounced off the rump of a Winchester horse.

"What's it going to take to get a goal past these guys?" Daisy groaned as they prepared for another lineout.

There was less than a minute left to play and unfortunately the game was going the wrong way. The lineout had been won by the Winchester number four who struck the ball with a massive shot towards the goal posts.

Speeding after it, Emily pushed her mare into a flat gallop, her eyes fixed on the ball. What she hadn't noticed was the Winchester number four also galloping, and gaining on her with every stride. "Emily!" Daisy called to her. "Man on!"

As the Winchester rider pulled up alongside her, Emily looked terrified that she was about to be barged off the ball, and then, to everyone's surprise, she fought back! She pulled hard on her reins and urged Jocasta to the right, charging into her opponent, making room to take a perfect backhander on the polo ball, sending it straight back up the field, heading in the right direction at last. But with only seconds left on the clock!

"It's mine!" Georgie called. She pushed Princess into a gallop, chasing the ball down at the halfway line, hanging out of the saddle like an acrobat as she stretched out to take the ball with a sweep shot.

The ball flew down the centre of the field towards the goal posts and Alice saw her chance to score. There were riders swarming around the goal mouth, but Alice took her chance. She lifted her stick to set up the shot. Daisy was running interference for her, blocking the Winchester number one.

Alice swung her stick back, but it was hooked by the Winchester number three.

"Oi! Get off!" Alice yelled. She yanked her stick free and spun Desiray round on her hocks to block the Winchester rider off the ball. Outplayed, the Winchester number three wasn't about to let a goal happen now. He rode his mare straight into Desiray, and at the same time he stuck out his arm, deliberately elbowing Alice square in the stomach.

Taken off guard by the blow, Alice doubled over completely and toppled off Desiray's back like a sack of wet cement.

"Foul!" Daisy raised a stick. As the riders from both teams were crowded in front of the goal, Georgie couldn't see Alice at all. Then the goal mouth cleared, and she saw Desiray. The mare was standing over Alice, who was sprawled motionless on the ground.

"Alice!" Georgie shouted. And then, like a death knell, came the sound of the bell that marked the end of the final chukka.

Chapter Sixteen

*I*f the Winchester number three was expecting to get away with his foul he clearly hadn't counted on Daisy. As the bell sounded, she leapt off her horse and stormed across the field like a banshee waving her mallet.

It took both Georgie and Emily to hold her back.

"Let me go!" Daisy demanded. "He's got it coming!"

"Daisy, urghhh, stop it!" Georgie was grappling with her while Emily took her mallet. "You can't just attack another player!"

"Why? Because I'll get disqualified?"

"No! Because he's three times your size and he'll cream you!"

"I don't care! Did you see what he did?" Daisy was furious. "He could have killed Alice!"

Alice, meanwhile, was only just coming round. The fall must have knocked her out cold and by the time she woke up the first face she saw was Cameron's. He had raced to her side and was cradling her in his arms. "Don't move, Alice," Cam was insisting. "They're getting an ambulance."

"No!" Alice said. "No ambulance. I have to finish the game…"

"Alice," Cam said softly, "the game is over. Just lie back down and wait for the paramedics."

"No, we can still win it," Alice insisted. "Help me up. Where's my pony?"

She struggled to her feet, still wobbly and grabbed Desiray's reins. "Come on!" she insisted. "Give me a leg up!"

"Alice," Cameron shook his head, "the bell has gone."

Alice ignored him and put her foot in the iron and sprang back up into the saddle.

"The bell sounded *after* I fell," she said to Cameron.

"And I was fouled by the Winchester number three, which means we're due a penalty shot. So it's not over yet."

Alice was right. The bell had sounded, but that didn't mean that the match had ended. The referee still had the power to hand out a penalty – and he was using it. He rode up to Georgie. "Get your girls back on their horses," he told her. "That was a direct foul on your number three. I'm giving you an undefended penalty from the thirty-yard mark. Choose a rider from your team to take the shot."

"See?" Emily said to Daisy. "Aren't you glad now that you didn't thump him? We're still in with a chance!"

Georgie mounted up and rode over to Alice. "Are you feeling up to taking the shot?"

Alice shook her head. "I want to say yes, but to be honest, I'm still seeing two polo balls instead of one!"

"Emily? Daisy? Do you guys want to take it?"

Emily shook her head. "You're the captain, Georgie. It's yours."

"She's right," Daisy agreed. "The captain should take it. Go even the score with those numnahs!"

As Georgie rode Princess forward to the thirty-yard line, she felt the eyes of the Blainford Academy upon her. Half the school was up in the grandstands right now watching her. The scoreboard stood at five-four in favour of the Winchester Reserves. If she got this penalty shot through the posts then they would be tied. If she missed, then her team and her school would lose.

"No pressure though, Princess," Georgie murmured to the mare beneath her.

The referee set the ball on the line and Georgie pressed Princess into a canter, going up into two-point position as she turned the mare round in a circle so that she had a run-up towards the ball.

In the stands the Blainford pupils were clapping along and chanting the school song as she cantered:

Bay, dun, dapple-grey, Blainford take it all the way!
Whip, spur, martingale, Blainford girls never fail!
We're here! We're true! We're silver and we're blue!
All-stars! All-stars! All-stars!

There was something strangely energising about having the shouts and cheers of hundreds of students behind her as she approached the ball. Princess felt it too. The mare was like a coiled spring and Georgie had to steady her back so they wouldn't overshoot the mark. As she prepared to swing at the ball she tried to remember everything that she'd been taught over the past few months, to keep her pace rhythmical, shoulders relaxed and her arm loose and soft. She was right on the thirty-yard line when she took a deep breath, swung back and struck the ball with a resounding crack.

The line was straight and true and the roar from the crowd came up as the ball flew perfectly dead centre between the posts. It was a goal!

Georgie cantered back to her team mates, her polo stick held up over her head as the ref's whistle blew.

As the girls hugged in joy, the Winchester players remained motionless on their horses, standing behind the goal line.

"What's up with the four horsemen of the apocalypse?" Daisy pointed at them. "What are they waiting for?"

"Yeah!" Emily said. "The game is over – it's a tie!"

Alice shook her head. "You can't finish a game on a tied score. There's going to be a rundown."

The rundown was the ultimate polo tie-breaker. To

decide the outcome of the match, each team lined up behind their opponents' goal line and sprinted from one end of the field to the other with the ball.

"You have to get all four of your players and your ball across your goal line to win," Alice explained as the girls lined up behind the goal posts.

"Do all four of us have to do it?" Georgie asked Alice pointedly. "A minute ago you couldn't even see straight!"

"I'm fine," Alice insisted. "I don't need to see straight to gallop – Desiray knows the way!"

"That number three better watch out," Daisy muttered. "I'm planning to take a swing at him on the halfway line with my mallet as he goes past."

"Daisy!" The girls all reacted.

"I'm joking!" Daisy said. "I don't want to risk giving him a penalty!"

As the girls lined up behind their goal line, Georgie rode over to Emily.

"You're going to take the first shot off the line," she told her. "You've got the best arm of any of us. Hit it as far as you can and then Daisy will ride it down to take the next stroke. OK?"

"OK," Emily looked terrified. At the other end of the field the Winchester squad were moving into formation and in the grandstands the Blainford students were starting up the school chant again as the girls took their places.

On the line, Princess was getting worked up with excitement. The mare went up on her hind legs and at that moment the whistle blew.

Alice and Daisy broke into a gallop as Emily eyed up the polo ball like a pro-golfer.

"Just hit the thing!" Georgie bellowed. "Let's go!"

Emily swung her mallet back and smashed the ball so hard it flew halfway down the field. Georgie let the reins go and Princess surged forward, her strides swallowing the ground.

Up ahead she could see Daisy strike the ball as she crossed the centre of the field with the Winchester riders charging at her from the other direction.

Daisy and Alice had the lead, but Emily was making up the time she'd lost at the start line, urging her mare on, asking for more speed.

Georgie stood up in her stirrups, leaning forward over

Princess's neck. Until now, Georgie had always assumed that Riley hadn't wanted the mare because she was too slow to be a racehorse, but as they powered down on the halfway line, she realised she had been wrong. Princess was stretching out, her long, flat strides betraying her Thoroughbred bloodlines. Georgie was pretty sure that she had never gone this fast on a horse before.

There was a sickening moment at the centre line when Georgie realised she was heading straight for one of the Winchester players going in the opposite direction. She shut her eyes and pulled Princess hard to the right, hoping that the Winchester rider wouldn't go the same way. Two strides later, she opened her eyes and she was out the other side and heading for the finish line. The rundown would be close – the Winchester Players were galloping as hard out as the Blainford girls. They must be neck and neck.

At the quarter marker Georgie had caught up to the other girls as Alice caught the polo ball with a neat shot, edging it closer to the line.

The sight of the ball zipping ahead of them seemed

to energise Princess. The mare chased it down and Georgie arced her stick back and struck the ball with a clean thwack, shooting it over the line before galloping the last yards with her three team mates at her side as they stormed to the finish.

As the four girls rode across the line they had their backs to the Winchester Reserves and couldn't see whether they had beaten them or not. But they didn't need to – an unmistakeable roar went up from the stands. The school was on their feet and the chant began. "All-Stars! All-Stars!"

Blainford Academy had won the Low Goal Bluegrass Cup.

✳

Two days later, Georgie climbed the stairs that led to Mrs Dickins-Thomson's office once again. She had been summoned by the headmistress, although she had no idea why. They were no longer in trouble for leaving the school grounds without permission to compete in the qualifiers. Winning the match had conveniently erased any misdemeanours as far as Mrs

Dickins-Thomson was concerned. How could you be in trouble when you were the school's heroes?

Yesterday, at assembly, Georgie, Alice, Emily and Daisy had been called on to the stage of the Great Hall and presented with their winners' trophy and their school 'colours' in polo – a badge that indicated sporting excellence of the highest order. It was the second time in the history of the Blainford Academy that any girl had been awarded this honour.

"I believe you knew the last girl who won this," Mrs Dickins-Thomson said to Georgie with a smile as she pinned the badge on her collar. "Like mother, like daughter."

Georgie had phoned Lucinda that night back in Little Brampton to tell her the news.

"Your mother would be so proud," Lucinda said to Georgie. And then she added, "Well, I suppose I shall need to turn one of the grazing paddocks into a polo field now so that you'll have somewhere to train the next time you come home for hols!"

The groundbreaking win at the Bluegrass Cup by the Badminton team had sparked even more enthusiasm amongst the Blainford girls' boarding houses and now that Badminton had secured the polo string on a permanent basis Stars of Pau and Adelaide were also barracking to start teams of their own.

"We are trailblazers!" Alice announced as they walked back up the driveway to dinner that evening. "I feel like Germaine Greer!"

"Is she a famous polo player?" Emily asked.

Alice sighed. "Look her up on Wikipedia, Emily!"

"I'm giving JP my dessert at dinner tonight," Daisy announced, "as a thank-you for being my stick chick."

"You owe Cameron more than a dessert," Georgie said to Alice. "Did you see the way he raced over to you when you fell off?"

"Well, I didn't actually see it because I was out cold."

"He totally wigged out when he thought that you were hurt," Emily said. "It was very romantic the way he held you in his arms."

Alice didn't look impressed. "Most of my romantic dreams about Cam don't involve the whole school watching."

"But it showed how much he cares about you!" Emily

said. "Maybe he's going to realise at last that you're more than just good friends."

"I'm not holding my breath," Alice said. "And I'm not giving him my dessert – not tonight at least. It's chocolate pudding night!"

✳

The excitement had settled down two days later by the time Georgie received the summons from the headmistress. As she climbed the stairs to Mrs Dickins-Thomson's office, Georgie was hoping she wasn't in some kind of trouble.

Her suspicions grew worse when she rounded the landing of the stairs and came face to face with a furious Heath Brompton.

"Parker!" he snapped. "This is all your fault!"

"I'm sorry, sir?"

"You should be sorry, Parker!" the polo master continued. "It appears that your stellar win has caused quite a stir. There's a queue of girls wanting to join the polo classes."

Georgie tried to suppress a grin.

"It's not funny, Parker!" Mr Brompton said. "Because of you Mrs Dickins-Thomson has just informed me that she has plans to expand the polo faculty. She's appointing a head of department."

Georgie was confused. "Uhh, congratulations, sir?"

"Don't be facetious, Parker!" Heath Brompton fumed.

"I'm sorry, sir?"

"She has appointed a new head," Heath Brompton said. "And *her* name is Arabella Chandler."

Georgie had to fight to suppress the grin that was spreading on her face. "I'll see you in class next week, sir?"

"Don't count on it!" Heath Brompton shot back as he pushed past her and disappeared down the stairs.

"Come in, Miss Parker!" Mrs Dickins-Thomson said brightly when she heard Georgie's tentative knock at her door. "We were just talking about you!"

Georgie had assumed that the 'we' the headmistress was referring to was herself and Mr Brompton. She was surprised when she entered the room and found that there was someone else in there sitting with the headmistress.

"Miss Kelly and I have just been having a very interesting conversation about your future," Mrs Dickins-Thomson said. "Haven't we, Tara?"

Tara Kelly turned to Georgie. "I was just saying that considering your excellent performance on the polo field this term, I would be very keen to have you back in my class next term," Tara said. "That is, if you're willing to give up the polo option and take up cross-country again?"

Georgie looked dumbstruck.

"I understand that your success as a polo rider means that you may want some time to think about it," Tara continued.

"No!" Georgie said.

Tara looked taken aback. "You mean you don't want to rejoin the cross-country class?"

"No!" Georgie said. "I mean, no, I don't need time to think! I would love to come back. Yes, please!"

Tara laughed. "I'll see you in my first class next term, Georgie. It's good to have you with us again."

✳

As she walked to the stables that evening, the weather was freezing cold, but Georgie didn't care. She dug her hands deep into the pockets of her non-regulation Barbour as she turned past the gateway of Burghley House and headed for the stable block.

The polo ponies had already been given their feed for the evening, but she wanted to look in on Princess. Tara had been right – the grey mare had been a total star in the rundown. She was so impressive that the gruff Winchester captain had asked Georgie if she would consider selling the mare to him, but Georgie had politely refused.

The truth was, she had been considering giving the mare back to Riley. She had felt awful about the trade they had made. Riley had clearly sacrificed one of his best horses in exchange for the total untrainable nightmare Marco. It was a sweet and noble thing for him to do, but Georgie couldn't possibly keep Princess.

"I want to swap back," she had told Riley in the truck on the way home from the Frankfort polo grounds.

"No way!" Riley grinned at her.

"But it's not fair," Georgie said. "I really appreciate

what you did for me, but I can't leave you lumbered with Marco."

"Well I'm not trading back," Riley said. "Marco won his first stakes race last weekend. I'm training him up for the Oaks."

Georgie couldn't believe it. "Are you serious?"

"Totally," Riley said. "That horse is going to pay my way through college."

It turned out that wilful Marco had come in three lengths ahead of the field and Riley was now fielding offers from major stables who all wanted to buy him.

So Princess remained Georgie's favourite pony in the string and she had sat proudly astride her when the Blainford Girls' Polo Team photo was taken. Georgie couldn't believe it when Mrs Dubois informed them that Mrs Dickins-Thomson was planning to include the picture in the wall of fame in the school dining hall. Georgie had to admit that she loved the idea of a portrait of her team staring down on Kennedy Kirkwood and Conrad Miller as they ate their dinner.

After she looked in on Princess, Georgie left the polo stalls and headed down to the main stable block at the back of the school. She had moved Belle back in with the eventers now. The mare's hogged mane was beginning to grow back and although it was currently in a difficult in-between stage with the hairs sticking up like the ruff of a Roman centurion's helmet it wouldn't be long until the mare looked like her old self again.

"Another month or two and I'll be able to plait it," Georgie murmured to Belle as she leaned across the stable door and stroked the mare's broad, bay neck. "And by the time we're back in cross-country class, you'll look just like you did before."

Belle nickered appreciatively, as if she too was pleased at the news that they were going back to Tara Kelly's class. In a way, Georgie suspected that the mare had missed jumping as much as she did. She was too well-bred and too brave over fences to live life as a polo pony. As for Georgie, she would keep playing polo. But cross-country had always been the dream, and now she was back in Tara's class where she belonged.

Riley had turned out to be right – hadn't he always said that she would find a way back into Tara's class?

It was ironic that Riley had been so determined not to get involved with a Blainford girl – yet if it wasn't for him, Georgie would never have survived her last term at the academy.

OK, maybe it wouldn't be easy trying to date a boy who didn't belong to Blainford, but Georgie didn't care. She had spent the past term so confused about her feelings, but now she knew. It was him. It had always been him. After all they had been through, she just hoped that Riley felt the same way.

It was getting dark as she left the stables and walked back down the driveway. She could see the lights of Badminton House, and there on the road, right outside the front door, she could see the front headlights of a red pick-up truck. Her heart raced as the door of the truck opened and Riley got out. He'd been waiting for her.